MW01136354

Loving

Misty

Stone Knight's MC
Book 3

Megan Fall

Loving Misty
Published by Megan Fall

This book is a work of fiction. Any similarities to real people,
places, or events are not intentional and are purely
the result of coincidence. The characters, places, and events
in this story are fictional.

Copyright © 2018 by Megan Fall. All rights reserved

All rights reserved. This publication may not be reproduced,
distributed, or transmitted in any form without the express
written consent of the author except for the
use of small quotes or excerpts used in book reviews.

Dedication

To my husband
Craig
Who has always stuck by my side!

Contents

Chapter One
Misty

Misty carefully lifted her hand and felt across the top of the bathroom counter. Finally, she located her brush. Picking it up, she ran it through her long golden brown hair. She loved her hair, as it was the same colour as her mothers, and wished with everything she had that she could see it now.

Almost two years ago, she was driving to dinner with her parents. An impaired driver crossed the median and hit their car head on. Both her parents were killed instantly. She suffered quite a few cuts and bruises, but the most damage she received was to her head.

The back of her head slammed into the side window from the impact. The doctors told her she had significantly damaged the optical cortex. It caused her to suffer a partial blindness, meaning she is only able to see shadows and shapes.

The blow also caused headaches and dizzy spells. The doctors told her that there is no indication of how long the blindness could last. For some people it last days, others months or a year, and in some cases it never returns at all.

For her, she figured it was permanent. She still suffered the headaches and dizziness, only not as often, but since the accident, her sight hadn't improved at all. She was just as bad off now as she was when it happened.

She sometimes wished she was completely blind. The shadows only frustrated her and made it harder. The light hurt her eyes too, so she had taken to wearing sunglasses when she was out during the day.

Her brother Noah was a marine and been stationed in Afghanistan at the time. He was given leave to come home and attend the funeral. He also stayed long enough to make sure she was settled, then he was under orders to go back. He had to sell her parents house, to pay for the funerals and her medical bills, so he had moved her into his apartment. Since he was engaged to Carly, and she was their only family, Misty was now in her care.

Unfortunately, as soon as Noah left, Carly showed her true colours. She hated being Misty's caregiver and was constantly making it known. Plus, Misty was pretty sure Carly was seeing someone else behind her brothers back. Her brother only called about once or twice a month, and with him stationed in the middle of a battlefield, Misty knew she couldn't burden him with her problems. She put up with Carly's abuse and went on with her life.

Most days she sat at home and read on the Braille book reader her brother had bought her. She also liked to pop in her ear buds and listen to music on her iPod. Sometimes she ventured to the park down the street, but even that was difficult.

Today, Carly insisted on driving her to a coffee shop, and she planned on leaving her there while she went to run a couple errands. She promised she would only be about forty-five minutes, then she would pick her up and take her back home. Misty didn't really want to go, but she knew she needed to start getting out more.

That's why she had been searching for her hairbrush. She kept begging Carly not to move her things, but of course Carly told her she needed to clean, and to do that she had to put things away. Sometimes it took Misty an hour to find her things after Carly cleaned. It was frustrating and some days she even shed a few tears. Misty knew Carly did it on purpose, just to upset her.

Misty finished in the bathroom, and grabbed her cane, heading out to living room in search of Carly. She finally found her waiting by the door as Carly liked to ignore her when she called. Misty sighed and followed her out of the apartment and downstairs to her car. She was careful on the stairs as Carly never helped.

Once they had made it to the car, she opened the door and climbed in.

She hoped her afternoon was better, but didn't have very high hopes. Life just wasn't what she expected it to be anymore, and she was beginning to lose hope of it ever getting better.

Chapter Two
Misty

Misty sat at the table in the coffee shop, drinking her tea. She figured she had been waiting about two hours now for Carly, but she couldn't see the clock to know for sure. She was actually getting nervous, wondering what she would do if Carly actually left her here. She wouldn't put it past her. Carly had made her wait longer than she told her before, but this was well beyond that.

Misty started to shuffle back and forth in her seat. She had drank two cups of tea, as Carly had told the waitress to bring her a second cup once the first cup was gone, before she had left.

Now however, the tea was starting to move through her, and she knew it wouldn't be long before she'd be desperate for a bathroom.

She shifted again and cringed when she heard her cane hit the ground. Leaning over, she patted the surrounding floor, searching for it. With no luck, she huffed in agitation. She knew this day would be bad, but this was humiliating.

Suddenly, there was a shadow at her side. She heard the person bend down and pick up her cane. "If you hold out your hand, I can place the cane in it, and then you can put it where it's easy for you," a female said.

Misty nodded and did as told. Instantly, the cane was placed in her hand. "Thank you," she told the kind woman. She heard a chair scrape as the woman sat down.

"I don't mean to intrude," she said. "But I noticed you've been sitting here for an awfully long time. Do you need a ride somewhere?"

Misty smiled at the kindness. "No, actually my roommate should be along shortly. She ran some errands, and I guess it's taking her longer than she expected."

"I'm Ali," the woman said. "Do you mind if I sit with you, while you wait? I really don't like sitting alone, and I have to wait for my husband, anyway."

"Sure, I'm Misty, she told her, not wanting to sit by herself any longer either.

"Do you mind me asking if you were born blind," Ali asked. And that was the start of her new friendship. She told Ali all about the accident as well as her prognosis, and all about her brother Noah. She told her about Carly as well, but left out all the bad stuff. Ali listened and seemed to really care about her answers.

Misty starting wiggling again, desperate to go to the bathroom. Then, she heard the chair scrape as Ali got up. "I've had a bottle of water, and I need to use the restroom, do you want to come with me before our rides get here?"

Misty couldn't get out of her seat fast enough. "Yes please," she said. She sighed in relief as Ali took her arm and led the way. In the bathroom,

Ali was amazing. She led her to a free stall and helped her inside, then showed her where the toilet paper was. When she was done, Ali was there again leading her to the sink. This time she casually told her which side the soap was on and how many steps to the paper towels.

Misty couldn't believe how easy Ali made everything. She didn't make her feel like she was disabled at all and talked to her like a normal person. When they got back to the table, she helped her grab her things so they could wait outside.

She was surprised when Ali asked for her phone so that she could put her number in. Noah had bought her a special phone with braille on it, so she could use it without needing to see it. She told Ali to enter her number under three and waited while Ali did as she asked. Then she heard Ali's phone ding, as she called herself so she could have her number.

Then, she cringed as she heard Carly call her name. She sounded extremely impatient and almost upset with her. Ali gave her a quick hug, telling her they'd talk soon. Then, she reluctantly made her way to Carly and got in the car.

She was thrilled she had a new friend and really hoped she heard from Ali again. She really liked the woman and hoped this could be the beginning of something positive for her.

Chapter Three
Misty

It had been two weeks since Misty met Ali. They had only talked on the phone once since that day, but Misty hadn't realized that she was pregnant. Apparently, she was due any day now, and her husband didn't want her far away from him. She loved that for her new friend and hoped one day she could have the same thing.

Carly had been busy this week and hadn't been around much. She worked full time as a receptionist at a dental office, but Misty had no idea where she went in the evenings. It worried her, but in all honesty, she liked it when she was gone. Things were easier without the added stress of always worrying what kind of mood she would be in the day.

With her busy too, she didn't have as much time to clean. That meant things weren't being moved as much, which Misty was extremely relieved about. Sometimes, Carly would move the furniture, and Misty would have bruises for a week as she learned the new layout. She could hear Carly snickering when she hit something and knew she did it on purpose.

Misty really hoped her brother came home soon. She hadn't seen him since the accident, and although he'd called her quite a bit, it wasn't the same. She prayed that he'd get to see the side of Carly that she saw. She didn't want her brother hurt, but she didn't want him miserable either.

Misty jumped as Carly called her name, she hadn't even heard her enter the room. "It's nice out, and you've been hiding inside too long. Come on, we're going for a drive," she ordered.

Misty signed, but didn't want to deal with Carly's attitude if she said no. She reached for her cane, and followed her out the door.

"Where are we going," she asked Carly, as they made their way down the stairs and outside.

"It's early evening," she said. "I thought we could go for a walk down by the lake, maybe sit at one of the picnic tables for a bit."

They'd reached the car, so Misty opened the door and climbed in. A walk by the lake would be nice, but she didn't trust Carly. She had learned that she had to be on her toes whenever they left the house.

The lake was only a five minute drive, so it went really quick. Misty got out, loving the feel of the breeze from the lake on her face. Maybe things would go well this time, she thought. She listened for Carly's footsteps and followed her to the water.

Misty was extremely familiar with the lake. Before her accident, she used to take a ton of pictures. She loved scenery, and this was one of her favourite spots. She had gotten so good that her brother had set her up with her own website. She framed her photographs and sold them, even taking requests for certain shots.

She missed it terribly and was worried about her website. She hadn't seen it since the accident, and Carly refused to help her. Maybe Ali would be willing to take a look at it for her. She didn't have any new photos, but she could reprint some of her favourites, and try to sell them. She hated not being able to help out her brother with the expenses.

Her and Carly were sitting at a picnic table, enjoying the weather, when Carly's phone suddenly rang. She tried to listen, but Carly got up and walked away, obviously not wanting her to overhear.

When Carly came back, she told her. "That was a friend of mine. I need to go, so you'll have to walk back."

"What," Misty asked horrified. There was no way she could walk home. "Drop me off on the way," she pleaded.

"I don't have time," Carly said with agitation in her voice. "Just walk straight out to the road and follow it home. You can see shadows, so you should be fine." Then Carly turned and walked away. Misty called her name, but she was ignored. As she listened, the car started and pulled out of the lot.

Misty was near tears. It was getting later, making it almost impossible for her to even see shapes. How in the world was she supposed to find her way home?

Chapter Four
Misty

Trike put the last screw in the change table and turned to Dragon, "done," he bragged.

"Fucker," Dragon bellowed, throwing down his wrench. "I thought you were just fast at running, you're fucking fast at everything," he complained.

Ali snickered from the corner, and Dragon glared at her, causing her to laugh. Trike shook his head at the two of them. They had gone through so much together that they deserved this happiness. Trike was glad he had gotten so close to the two of them, he was proud to call them friends.

Ali was about two weeks away from having their baby, and Dragon hadn't put the baby furniture together yet. Of course, he didn't want to do it all himself, so Dragon had called him and bet him fifty bucks he could get the crib together faster than Trike could get the change table together. It was a bet he had just lost.

Trike put his hand out. "Pay up brother," he told him. "Then I'll help you finish putting the crib together."

"Deal," Dragon instantly agreed, pulling the money out of his pocket and shoving it in his hand. Trike smiled as he pocketed it, not admitting that he would have put the table together for free.

Trike loved their cabin, he thought it was perfect. It was small, cozy and sat secluded at the end of the property. They had built it on a lake, and the views were amazing. Steele's cabin was next door, but you couldn't see it for the trees.

Trike was so taken by the cabins that he had started his own. He didn't have a woman yet, which was a requirement, but Steele owed him for saving Cassie's life and had pulled some strings with the club. He was building his on the other side of Steele's. The cabin was framed, but not much was done on the inside. He was taking his time as he had to stay in the clubhouse until he found his a woman of his own.

Trike loved the club and his brothers. Prospecting was the best thing he'd ever done. His own parents were older and had retired to Florida, pretty much leaving him on his own. Trike was still young, at twenty-four, and there was no way he was living in a retired couples house in Florida. He stayed here and met Preacher, the rest was history.

Ali's phone started ringing, startling her, and she reached to answer it. Trike only caught half of the conversation. It sounded like someone was in trouble, and Ali was more frantic the longer the conversation lasted. Dragon was by her side instantly, picking his wife up and sitting down with her on his lap.

Finally, she hung up and turned to Dragon. "Do you remember I told you about that girl I met in the coffee shop that day, Misty," she asked him. He nodded, and she continued. "Her roommate left her stranded at the lake," she cried. "It's dark, and she can't figure out how to get home. She's really scared Jaxon, we need to go find her."

"I don't understand," Trike said. "It's not that dark, that she can't walk to the road and find her way home."

"She's blind brother," Dragon told him.

"Fuck me," Trike exclaimed. Why would the roommate leave her like that," he asked in annoyance.

"The roommate's a spawn from hell," Ali seethed. "Someone needs a cup of holy water and a bible to get rid of that one," she told them.

Trike stood. "I'll go," he said instantly. "It's the lake just off Main Street, the one with the picnic tables?" Ali nodded, so Trike stood, heading for the door. He turned back to Ali before he left. "I'll find her," he told her. "That girl will be in her own bed tonight, I promise." Then he hurried out the door, heading for his hog.

In seconds he was roaring down the road and headed for the lost blind girl. He'd keep his promise to Ali. He'd make sure that girl was safe.

Chapter Five
Misty

Misty was terrified. It was getting darker and she couldn't see at all. She had tried to find the road, but it was impossible. She had tripped several times, had ran into both a picnic table and a tree, and had somehow fallen into the lake. That had scared her, but she had luckily only fallen to her knees, so it was easy to get out of.

Misty had finally given up and was now sitting on the ground with her knees pulled up to her chest. She jumped at every noise she heard, and she was crying. She had no idea that Carly could be so cruel. How could she just leave her here at night? She made her decision then and there, that the next time Noah called, she would tell him about Carly's treatment of her. She definitely couldn't live like this any longer.

Plus, she had no idea who Carly was hanging out with. She was barely home, and when she was, she made sure she was by herself. Carly didn't have many friends, but for some reason, Misty figured she didn't want her to know who it was she was hanging out with. Misty had a feeling she was cheating on her brother, but without her eyesight, she had no way to prove it.

Suddenly, there was a loud rumbling noise as a motorcycle approached. She listened as it got closer and stopped. Then she panicked, who would possibly be coming to the lake in the dark. She curled up into a tighter ball as she listened to what sounded like heavy boots stomp through the park.

When she heard her name being called, she was flabbergasted. She sat there in silence for a minute and listened to him call for her again. His voice was deep and growly, sending tingles through her body.

"Misty honey, please come out if you can hear me. I'm a friend of Ali's, and she asked me to help you. I need to make sure you get home safe," she heard him say.

Slowly, she picked up her cane and untangled her legs. She had been sitting on the cold ground for a while, and with her pant legs wet, she was stiff. She stood and came out from behind a tree. She hoped she was where he could see her because she didn't want to move very far. Tears still streamed down her face, and she couldn't stop the small sob that escaped.

She heard the footsteps approach and knew he had found her. She jumped, when he spoke from right in front of her.

"Oh honey," he said. "What a state you've got yourself in. Can I touch you," he asked.

She didn't know him, but she trusted Ali. If she sent the man, then he had to be a good one. She nodded, then squealed when he came close and wrapped his arms around her, pulling her into his massive chest. She gave up from pure fear and exhaustion and collapsed against him. He was huge next to her tiny frame, and she finally felt safe.

She heard him murmuring soothing words to her as he let her cry it out. When she finally calmed down, and got a hold of herself, he pulled back slightly.

"You're just a tiny thing, aren't you," he said. "I can feel your wet pants against my legs. You trying to go for a swim," he asked.

She finally smiled, but told him, "I got turned around and stumbled into the lake."

"Christ," she heard him murmur. "It's pretty dark out here, and I need to make sure you're okay. Can I take you home," he asked.

She nodded quickly and rattled off her address. He took her arm, and brought her close, as he headed back to his bike. He then put a helmet on her head and strapped it on.

"You ever been on a bike before," he questioned.

"My brother has a bike. I used to ride with him all the time," she told him.

He helped her on, then climbed on in front of her. "Hold on to me tight honey," he ordered her.

Suddenly, she got the crazy idea that she wanted to hold on to him forever, and not let go.

Chapter Six
Trike

Trike was completely taken with the cute blind girl. When she stepped out of the trees, he was shocked. She was short, with long brown hair. Even in the dark, he could see the red highlights throughout it. She was perfect in his eyes, and he struggled with the instant feelings he had for her. He knew immediately why Ali had sent him, and not Dragon. She was trying to set them up.

The poor girl looked terrified, and tears were streaming down her face. He had been shocked when she had allowed him to comfort her and then collapsed against him. She felt absolutely perfect in his arms, and he didn't want to let her go.

He was furious when she admitted she fell in the water. She could have drowned. She let him take her to his bike and had climbed on with complete trust in him. He had taken her cane and strapped it to the side of his bike.

Now her arms were wrapped around him, and her head was resting against his back. They arrived at her apartment way too quickly for his liking. He parked his hog, knocked the kickstand down and climbed off. He took her helmet off first, then grabbed her around the waist and lifted her off. He laughed as she squealed.

Trike took her arm and led her inside, and up the stairs. When they reached the door, he asked her for her keys. She pulled a chain out of her shirt and lifted it over her head, handing it to him. He unlocked the door and made sure to put it back in her hand.

He watched as she moved carefully to the couch, using her cane, then slumped down onto it. "How long have you lived here", he questioned her.

She glanced in his direction, then told him. "It's been two years, but my roommate keeps rearranging the future, so I can't memorize it."

He cursed, as he headed over to her. He made a note to find out more about this roommate later. He sat down next to her slowly, trying not to startle her.

"I need to make sure you're okay, but first I wonder if you could change into some shorts and a t-shirt. You're pretty wet, and I don't want you to get sick," he explained.

She nodded and got up, again slowly making her way around the furniture and heading down the hall. While she was gone, he pulled out his phone and called Ali. He explained that he had found her, and they were now at her place. He told her she was wet from falling in the lake, and the knee of her jeans had been ripped, but other than a few scrapes and bruises, she was okay. When he heard Misty coming back, he hung up.

Misty looked cute. She was wearing blue pyjama shorts and an oversized marine t-shirt. When he asked about the t-shirt, she explained about her brother fighting overseas. He had been jealous, but he realized he had jumped to conclusions. He noticed a huge scrape on her knee and some scratches near her feet. The palms of her hands were a bit scratched up too.

She directed him to her bathroom, and Trike came back with the first aid kit she had told him was there. She seemed to be really comfortable with him, so it made it easy for him to take care of her. He cleaned her knee and covered the cut with gauze. The scratches near her feet weren't bad, so he just cleaned them and applied some ointment, doing the same with her hands.

He left to put the first aid kit away, then picked up a blanket off her bed. He was surprised to see quite a few boxes in the corner, but decided to leave that one alone. When he came back into the living room, she was fast asleep. He smiled, then picked her up and carried her to her room. She snuggled in and leaned her head on his chest.

Once he had her settled in her bed, he stared at her a minute. He knew already that this tiny girl was worming her way into his heart. He was going to find more out about the roommate, and he was going to make sure this girl's life was easier. He had a feeling things were going to get difficult, but that was fine with him. He liked difficult, and he had a feeling this girl would be worth it.

Chapter Seven
Misty

Misty woke to a loud banging on the door. She climbed out of bed, grabbed her cane and made her way to the door.

"Who's there," she asked.

"Misty, its Trike, let me in," she heard him respond.

She panicked for a minute. Being blind and not being able to see, made it really hard to know how she looked. She ran her hands down her hair, hoping that helped, then unlocked the door and opened it. She could see his shape as he walked in and wondered what he looked like.

She smelled baked goods, and shut the door, following him to the couch. She heard him sit, so she sat carefully beside him, then bags shook as he pulled things out.

"I didn't know what you liked, so I got a bit of everything," he told her. "I have muffins, carrot, bran, blueberry and chocolate chip. I have a couple croissants, and a couple bagels, plain and apple cinnamon." Then there was silence for a minute. "Oh, and I have apple juice and orange juice. I don't give much for coffee," he said.

She was floored. "You brought all this to share with me," she asked.

"Well ya, and what we don't eat I figure we can stash in your room for later," he told her. She smiled up at him and nodded.

When he asked her what she wanted, she immediately told him blueberry muffin and apple juice. He handed it to her, and she dug in.

"I'll remember what you picked for next time," he promised. She got excited about that, really glad that there was going to be a next time. "I was hoping you wouldn't pick the chocolate chip muffin," he said. "I really wanted it."

She laughed at him, amused by his sweet tooth. She knew he rode a motorcycle, but he didn't act the type. He was really sweet and caring when she figured he'd be rough and slightly rude.

"Do you ride by yourself, or do you belong to a club," she asked.

"I belong to a club and have for about a year and a half now. I'm pretty much the newest, and youngest member at twenty-four. It's the best thing I've ever done, and wouldn't change a thing. And before you ask, we're all good guys. We don't do anything illegal, unless it's because we're protecting one of our own, and we don't ride around causing trouble."

"Okay," Misty told him.

"Okay," he repeated. "That's it."

"Yep," she told him. "You being a biker doesn't bother me. My brother rides, and he's a marine. He talked about joining a biker club when he comes home, just so he has the same close bond he has now."

"Wow, we could use someone like him. And we have a few ex-military men in our ranks already, so he'd fit right in."

"So Trike, can I ask what your real name is? I feel funny calling you Trike," she asked cautiously.

"Trike's the name my club brothers gave me. They said that I was so young, I should have training wheels on my bike." She giggled at that one. "My real name's Brody," he told her.

"I really like Brody. Can I call you that instead of Trike," she asked.

"I'd love that," he told her, and she could hear the happiness in his voice. "Now, go shower quick, and make sure to wear a pair of jeans. I'm taking you out for a while," he stated.

She begged to know where they were going, but he wouldn't budge. He promised to be a good boy and stay where he was, unless of course she needed any help. She laughed again, and realized she was laughing a lot around him, and she really liked it.

She hurried to her room to shower, excited to see where they would end up. She really liked Brody, and she really hoped he liked her too.

Chapter Eight
Trike

Trike heard the shower shut off and knew Misty wouldn't be much longer. He headed for the kitchen and immediately starting going through cupboards. Finally, he found a container big enough to hold the baked goods he had bought. He transferred them to it, then threw out the bag.

As he was leaving the kitchen Misty came walking down the hall. He moved heavily towards her, trying to make enough noise so she'd know he was there. When she looked in his direction, he asked if he could put the baked good in her room. She readily agreed, so he moved past her and then placed them on her nightstand.

He came back out, to find her sitting in an armchair close to the door. She was in the middle of lacing her running shoes, and even without seeing them, she was doing them up perfectly. He told her where he left the baked goods and then took her hand. She already had her cane, so they headed out.

He closed the door behind her and turned to watch her take her key from around her neck and hand it to him. He smiled happily as he locked the door and placed the chain back around her neck. Then he kissed her head and took her hand again to lead her down the stairs.

They were almost down to the bottom, when the front door of the building was thrown open, and a girl rushed in. She was tall, at least five-eight or five-nine, slim, and had medium length blonde hair.

She looked up and saw him, and he cringed at the seductive smile that graced her lips. Instantly, she threw her hip out and leaned against the wall. The action caused her shirt to ride lower on her chest and he could see the top of her red bra. He quickly looked away in disgust.

"Well hello there handsome. I've never seen you here before. Did you just move in, or are you here to see someone, maybe me," she purred.

Trike opened his mouth to respond to the ridiculous comment, but was pushed aside by Misty.

"He's here to see me," she told the girl angrily. "Did you conveniently forget you're engaged, or have you broken it off and just not told my brother or me?"

In a flash the girls face changed, the seduction was gone, to be replaced with fury. "No, we haven't broken up. But as you are aware, your brothers been gone for almost two years this time. Phone calls every couple weeks aren't good enough. I can flirt, but if he doesn't get back soon, I'm going to do more than that," she threatened.

"And," she continued, "you're in my care. I don't think your brother would take too kindly to you hanging out with a biker. I have no idea where you were, to meet a man like this, but you better turn around and head back up those stairs."

Trike didn't even wait for Misty to reply, he let go of her hand and placed it on the railing, then turned and stomped down the two steps until he stood in front of the witch.

"Who the fuck do you think you are," he growled. "That girl may be staying with you, but in no way do you have any right to order her around. And for your information, she met me last night, when you dumped her at the lake in the dark. Now, I know you see my cut, so you know what I am. I'll be watching you, and so you realize what that means, the club will be watching you." He waited a minute as her brows drew together.

"This girl now has the clubs protection. She's starting to mean something to me, and I'd like to see where that heads. So, in no way would I fuck that up by messing with a bitch like you.

Now you can fuck off because I have somewhere I want to take my girl."

He turned and marched back up the stairs. Then he scooped up his pretty little blind girl, and carried her out of the building, ignoring the bitch who was still standing there with her mouth wide open.

Chapter Nine
Misty

Misty couldn't believe she was in Brody's arms again, as he carried her out to his bike. This was the one time, since she had lost her sight, that she really wished she could see. She wanted to see Brody. She knew he was a bigger man because she felt his muscles and body last night when he held her. But she wanted to see the colour of his hair and eyes and wanted to see how he dressed. She just wanted to see him.

She realized Brody had stopped walking and figured they were at his bike. Instead of putting her down though, he sat, and she found herself on his lap. "What's the matter, sweetheart? If that bitch does anything else to hurt you, I'll take care of it," he told her.

"I want to see you," she whispered.

He was silent for a minute, then told her "you can." He reached down and took her hand. Misty was confused when he put it in his hair.

"My hairs a dirty blond colour. It's a bit long and messy, kind of reminds people of surfer hair. My eyes are blue. I'd say more about them, but I don't know how to describe them. I don't have any scars or marks. I usually wear old, faded blue jeans and most of them have tears in the knee. I wear white, blue or black shirts. Today I have on a blue one, and I always wear my cut over it. And I wear heavy black biker boots."

She smiled at him, and a couple tears fell from her eyes. "Thank you," she said softly. "No one's ever taken the time to do that for me. For almost two years it's been blackness, with some shadows and shapes. You just gave me my sight back for a minute, and I'll never forget that."

"I have to kiss you," she heard Brody say.

Then he placed his hand on her cheek. She felt his breath on her cheek, then his lips touched hers. It was a soft kiss, and when she sighed he took advantage and thrust his tongue inside. She melted into him and touched her tongue to his. They kissed for a few minutes before he pulled back.

"Best kiss of my life," he told her.

 She smiled and repeated it back to him. Then she was up again, and they were off. He sat her on his bike and strapped her helmet on, then hocked on her cane and climbed on in front of her. Immediately, she wrapped her arms around him and held on tight. He squeezed her leg, then flicked the kickstand as he started the bike, and they were off.

She had no idea how long they drove for before he stopped. She always lost track of time when she rode with her brother too, she just enjoyed the ride so much. She felt Brody flip down the kickstand and then get off. He removed her helmet and stored it away, then he lifted her off.

She sniffed the air, smelling flowers. He took her hand and led her away from the bike. "Wait," she said. "My cane."

"I've got you sweetheart, trust me." When she nodded, he continued on. He led her into a building, telling her when there was a step, and when to turn. He made it so easy on her. Then they stopped, and he paid someone an admission fee, keeping hold of her hand the whole time.

Brody led her forward again and opened another door. She stepped through, and the smell was even stronger here.

"My mom used to bring me here," he told her. "It's a botanical garden. I know you can't see, but I figured you'd like the smells, as that's what I remember the most about this place."

She smiled the whole time he led her around the building. He explained in depth, the colours and sizes of the different plants and flowers. Again, he made it seem like she could see them, and some of them she recognized from before she lost her sight.

Near the end, she found her favourite flower, recognizing it by smell. When he saw it was the daisies, he was surprised by her choice, expecting it to be something fancier. She explained that the house she had grown up in was surrounded by daisies, so they reminded her of her parents.

When they left, an hour later, she had a daisy tucked behind her ear.

Chapter Ten
Trike

Two days had passed since he'd seen Misty, but they talked on the phone lots. He loved to hear her laugh. He told her all about how the bikers had decorated Dragon's and Steele's rooms, when they first brought their women to the compound.

He had plans to see her later, but for now, he was hard at work. He had decided to buckle down and get his cabin finished. Both Dragon and Steele warned him that things could move fast for him, just like it did with them. If he had to move Misty in, he didn't want her in the compound, so he was determined to power through the inside finishes.

Luckily, his brothers were willing to help. Dragon and Navaho were installing the kitchen cabinets and sink. Steele was working on the bathrooms, and Preacher was hooking up the washer and dryer. Dagger was beside him, grumbling about getting stuck with the worst job.

Trike had dragged him to a nursery and purchased as many daisies as he could. They were now busy planting them all around the cabin. He knew Misty wouldn't be able to see them, but she had recognized the smell of them the other day, so he knew she'd know they were there.

Furniture was another matter. Trike had seen her bedroom and knew she liked blue. He figured if he kept the cabin in blues and whites, it would be easy. He bought everything he would need, but added touches of the colours everywhere. He had laid a blue rug in the living room and bought white pillows for the couch. He bought a beautiful blue comforter for the bed that had white daisies in it. Blue towels were bought for the bathrooms.

He felt bad that Misty couldn't see it, but he was getting good at explaining things to her. He didn't want her to miss out. He was really getting excited about the possibility of moving in here one day with her and hoped things worked out for them.

The club had looked into Carly, after he got her name from Misty, but they came up dry. Carly came from a normal home life and worked as a receptionist. She did nothing illegal, except maybe spend too much on clothes and she was starting to frequent a bar in the area. She had admitted to being lonely, when Trike had seen her, so maybe she was headed there to wallow. They would check it out just to make sure.

When they looked into her bank account, they noticed a monthly amount was being deposited by the military. Trike figured that was Misty's brother, Noah, taking care of the bills. The brothers wanted to look into Misty as well, but he nixed that. Until he had a reason to dig into her life, he'd leave it alone. He was gaining her trust, and he didn't want to lose it.

They finished planting the flowers and stood up, wiping their hands on their dirty jeans. The flowers looked really nice, and Trike was thrilled. He knew he was falling hard for the pretty little blind girl, but he couldn't help it.

Steele had pulled him aside earlier, telling him to follow his heart. He had fallen for Cassie pretty much on sight too. She had suffered a different set of problems, and was married too, but Steele had stayed by her side. Now they were living together and Steele couldn't be happier. Bikers are different he explained, and sometimes things just move faster.

Trike completely agreed. He had only known Misty a short time, but he wanted her away from Carly, and living in the cabin with him as soon as possible. Even though they hadn't found anything on the bitch, she had rubbed him the wrong way. The girl had something going on, Trike just needed to figure out what it was.

Chapter Eleven
Misty

Misty got ready for her date with Brody. She pulled on a pair of jeans, and a pretty t-shirt. The neck was a deep v, and a bit lower than her regular t-shirts. She brushed her hair out and left it down, the way Brody liked it. She dug through the bottom of her closet and pulled out her old boots. They were black, with a low heal, and came up almost to her knees. She hadn't had them on since the accident, but she figured Brody would like them.

She grabbed her cell, threw some money and her ID in her pocket, and placed her necklace over her head with the key on it. Hoping she had everything she needed, she headed out to the living room. She heard the tv was on, so Carly was here somewhere.

She didn't even have to look for her because Carly came to her. She found her arm grabbed roughly, then she was dragged over to the chesterfield. When Carly sat down, she was forced down with her. She winced as Carly's fingernails dug in.

"Why are dressed like you're going out," she snarled.

"Because I'm going out," she told her calmly. She cried out when Carly shook her, digging her nails in deeper.

"If it's with that biker, you can forget it," she told her.

Misty grabbed onto Carly's fingers and tried to pry them off, but her grip was too strong. "Let go of me," she said as she kept pulling.

"Someone needs to knock some sense into you," Carly sniped. "You're disrespecting your brother, by dating a biker. That man's trash, and everybody knows it. I'm only looking out for you, like your brother asked."

Misty finally pulled her arm free and glared in Carly's direction. "I like him, and I'm going to continue seeing him. You can tell my brother if you like, but I'll be talking to him too. I think he'd like to hear about how you left me at the lake at night."

"Are you threatening me," Carly snarled. "Because I don't think you want to mess with me."

Misty was actually a little worried about what Carly would do, but she held her ground. "Why do you hate me so much," she asked.

"Because I didn't sign on to be a babysitter. I was supposed to marry your brother last year. He was in the process of buying a house when the damn accident happened. We were happy, and we were financially set. But, then he had to pay for the funerals, and for your medical bills, and where did that leave us," she said angrily.

"Now I'm living in this stupid apartment, he only sends me enough money to pay the bills, and I have to look after your disabled ass. On top off that, he's been gone almost two years. He should have left the stupid marines, and stayed home to look after you himself, or put you in a group home somewhere," she huffed.

Misty was floored. Carly pretty much blamed everything on the accident, and her. It didn't sound like she even loved Noah, it just sounded like he had promised her the life she wanted. She'd never hated anyone in her life, but right now she hated Carly.

She was knocked suddenly as Carly got up and pushed passed her. She heard her move about the room, then the front door slammed as she left. Misty slumped back against the cushions as she tried to figure out what to do. She knew Carly could made things difficult for her, but what choice did she have?

She didn't want to whine to her brother, but she knew there were some things he needed to know. She left a message on his phone, knowing it could be days before he got it. Then she sat there and tried to think of what she could do.

Nothing came to her. Being blind left her with few options, and until her brother came home, she was basically stuck. She really liked Brody, and with their relationship being so new, she refused to dump her problems on him. She'd have to figure this out on her own.

Chapter Twelve
Trike

Trike pulled up to Misty's apartment and dropped the kickstand. He noticed Carly stomping across the parking lot and jumping into her car. Seconds later, she peeled out of the parking lot. Trike shook his head at her attitude, then strode towards the front door.

Luckily, someone was leaving, so he slipped inside before the door shut. He headed up the stairs and rapped on his pretty girls door. When she asked who it was, he smirked and told her. He had to wait a few minutes before the door finally opened.

"Hi Brody," she said, as she moved to the side, so he could get in. She waited for a second and tilted her head, listening to his footsteps. When she figured he was in, she shut the door. She turned in his direction and gave him a half smile.

"Sorry I was slow, I had to get a sweater," she told him. He eyed her curiously. It was fairly warm out, and he didn't think she'd need the sweater.

"It's warm out, you may not need it," he told her.

She looked down and mumbled, "I'll be okay." Something wasn't right, Trike would bet dollars on that. She always smiled at him, but he had only gotten a half one today. And, even though he knew she couldn't see him, she wouldn't look at him directly.

"You okay, honey," he asked her carefully.

"I'm fine," she said. "Are you ready to go?"

He sighed, obviously she wasn't going to let him know what was going on. "Sure," he told her. He took her hand then and led her towards the door. He opened it, making sure she was out then closed it behind her. He smiled when she immediately pulled the key from around her neck and handed it to him.

He locked the door, then placed the key back on her neck. Taking her hand again, he led her down the stairs. Half way down, she stopped suddenly.

"I forgot my cane," she whispered in embarrassment. He smiled at her.

"You don't need it," he told her. Then he pulled her slightly and continued down the stairs.

When they reached the bike, he pulled out the helmet and strapped it on her head. Then he leaned down and gave her a soft kiss. She gasped in surprise, then placed her tiny hands on his chest and kissed her back.

"We're headed to the compound honey. The brothers are having a bonfire, and I thought you might enjoy it," he explained.

She looked up at him, "I'm not very good with new people," she told him. "It's hard because of my blindness."

"I promise not to leave your side," he told her. "And my brothers really want to meet you."

She nodded, but didn't say anything. He decided then and there, to make sure she had a good time tonight.

Something was going on, and he'd figure it out and fix it. The way Carly had left, he knew it had to do with her. He couldn't stand to see his girl sad, he was falling for her, and he wanted everything to be good for her.

They climbed on his hog, and he pulled out. Her arms were wrapped around him, and her head rested on his back. He squeezed her leg in happiness and pushed his bike just a little faster. He smirked when she held on tighter.

When he pulled up to the gate, a new prospect was there to let him in. This one had been screened and looked into for weeks before they let him in. No one would forget the last two prospects, who ended up being cut from the club. Through their actions, Steele had been shot and Cassie had been hurt. They had certainly learned their lesson after that.

Trike threw down the kickstand and took off Misty's helmet. He was worried about her, and he prayed tonight went well.

Chapter Thirteen
Misty

Misty felt Brody take her hand as he led her through the compound. She didn't want to be here. She wasn't good in crowds, and after her fight with Carly, she wasn't really up for socializing. She tried to put on a brave face, she just wanted to get through this and go home.

They walked for a bit, but because it was darker, it was really hard for her to see. Trike thankfully, was going slower, so that helped a lot. She could hear the bikers talking and laughing as she got closer. Then Trike stopped, and she looked in his direction surprised.

"Relax," he whispered in her ear, making her jump. "I've got you, this is the safest place you could be. Let go a bit and have some fun. I just want to see you happy tonight."

Then he kissed her head and started walking again. She felt bad, she knew Brody would know she wasn't in a good mood, and would try to help her. She'd have to try to enjoy herself, for him.

Finally, they reached the spot where the other bikers were hanging out. She squinted, as a bright light hurt her eyes. The glow distorted everything, and the shadows and shapes only looked bigger. She closed her eyes as a wave of dizziness hit her. Trike immediately pulled her close.

"What's wrong honey," he asked in concern.

She turned her body, so she was angled away from the campfire. "Nothing," she told him, "I'm fine."

She could hear him growl then. She squealed when he suddenly picked her up, walked a couple steps, then sat with her on his lap. She grabbed his shoulders quick to stop herself from falling.

"You're not fine," he told her angrily. "You just about fell over, and something's bugging you, and I know it has to do with Carly. I saw her storm away from the apartment."

Misty hung her head in defeat. "We had a bit of an argument before she left. It's nothing serious, it's just hard to be around each other all the time," she told him. She figured that would be enough of the truth.

"And the dizziness," he pushed.

"The fire's bright, and it distorts the shapes I see. That's what made me dizzy, it messes with my eyes," she explained. She still had her eyes closed, so the dizziness had almost gone away completely.

She heard Brody sigh, then he seemed to get an idea. "Dagger, can you go in my room and grab my sunglasses? I keep them on my dresser," he told someone.

"Sure," a man beside them replied. Then she heard him get up and walk away. She laid her head on Brody's shoulder and tried to relax. Today just wasn't turning out well at all.

A couple minutes later, she heard the man return. Then Brody was telling her to lift her head, and he was sliding a pair of huge wrap-around sunglasses on her face. They were really big, and slid a bit, but she appreciated the effort.

When she turned to the fire though, she was surprised to see that she hardly saw it. With the glasses so dark, all she saw was a faint glow. She couldn't believe how much they helped.

"Better," she heard Brody ask.

"Yes," she said immediately. "Thank you."

He kissed her head, then introduced her to Dagger, who was the one to get the glasses. Next she met Dragon, Navaho, Steele and Preacher and Ali, with about a dozen others. She had no idea how she was going to remember all those names, but the bikers were extremely friendly and welcoming.

Finally, she was able to relax and enjoy herself. Brody kept her on his lap the whole evening, and she loved it. She heard lots of stories about him and the club. Her favourite was the stories about the bikers putting a pink comforter in Dragons room.

When it was time to go, she gave her goodbyes, and promised to come back. Suddenly, someone grabbed her arm.

"You've got some blood on your sweater," she recognized Steele's voice, as he asked the question. "You okay?"

Great she thought as she tried to figure out how to answer.

Chapter Fourteen
Trike

Trike was immediately concerned when Steele mentioned there was blood on Misty's sweater. He spun her around so he could see. Sure enough, her light blue sweater had a couple drops of blood on it, up high on the sleeve. He held her hand as he carefully pushed the sweater off her shoulder.

He cursed when he saw the handprint, and what he was sure were fingernail holes in her arm. Luckily, Misty didn't fight him, as he got a good look at the marks.

"Those really need to be cleaned and bandaged," Steele told him.

Trike thought the same thing, but he wanted to know how she got them first. "What happened honey," he asked her.

"I told you, me and Carly got in an argument," she sighed. "When I turned to walk away, I tripped. Carly caught me, but she must have grabbed me too tightly."

Trike knew instantly that she was lying. He looked to his brothers, and could tell they felt the same way.

"Okay," he told her. "I have a first aid kit in my bathroom, I'll take you there and clean you up."

Then he slowly picked her up, not wanting to startle her. She wrapped her arms around his neck and settled in. Trike loved that, and gave her a quick kiss on the head, then he turned and headed for the clubhouse. He nodded his thanks to Navaho as he opened the door for them. Once inside, he moved down the hall to his room. He looked at the door, and started to shift Misty, but again Navaho was there opening the door for him.

"Jesus brother," he said in surprise. "You're like a god damned ghost. I didn't even hear you following us."

Navaho just smiled, then turned and walked away. Trike shook his head, then moved into the room. He carried his pretty little blind girl into the bathroom and set her on the counter. Then, he pushed her sweater further down her arm, so it was out of the way.

He opened a cupboard, got the first aid kit, and set it on the counter beside her. The first thing he did was grab an antiseptic wipe and clean the cut and the dried blood around it. The cuts were small, and there were clearly five nail holes. He put ointment on them, then grabbed the gauze and wrapped up her arm.

He explained what he was doing the whole time, he didn't want her surprised by anything he did. When he was done, he told her he wrapped her arm because five bandages would look ridiculous.

Trike liked having her in his room, and rather than take her home, he asked her to stay. He really wanted her to sleep in his arms tonight. She seemed really hesitant at first until he told her nothing would happen. He wanted her comfortable with him first.

She completely surprised him when she agreed. Happily, he grabbed her a clean toothbrush, and told her where to find everything. Then, he took off his t-shirt and laid it on the counter, telling her she could wear it to bed. As he closed the door, she smiled at him, and he felt like he was on top of the world.

He quickly undressed, leaving only his boxers on, and sat on the side of the bed to wait for her. About five minutes later she came out. He jumped up, and moved towards her, taking her hand and leading her back to the bed. Once she was safely in, he climbed in beside her, and pulled her close. She curled her tiny body into his side and laid her hand on his chest.

"This is the first time I've ever slept in the same bed as someone," she quietly admitted.

Trike beamed at her confession. "Well," he told her. "The way this is going, I'm pretty sure there's going to be a lot more nights like this one."

Then he tilted her head, giving her a slow, deep kiss. When he pulled away, he smirked at the dazed expression on her face. When she put her head back on his shoulder, it only took a minute for her to fall asleep. Trike watched her sleep for a while, then he too finally closed his eyes and fell asleep. But, he did it was a smile on his face.

Chapter Fifteen
Misty

Misty woke slowly, enjoying the feel of Brody's arms around her. She loved cuddling up with him, and she got a lot more sleep than she usually did. He must have felt her wiggling a bit, because his arms tightened around her.

"Morning honey", he whispered.

"Morning", she whispered softly back. "Thank you for letting me stay the night."

"Trust me", he told her. "It was all my pleasure, no hardship at all. Do you want a shower or anything, then we can grab some breakfast in the common room."

"No", she told him regretfully. "I'll stay for breakfast, but I need to shower at my place. My brother put up special handicap bars to help me. It would be really hard without them", she explained.

"I could shower with you", he said. "Then you could use me instead of the bars."

She giggled. "As much as I know I'd enjoy that, I'm not quite ready for it yet."

"Fine", she heard him say. "Rain check."

"Okay", she said giggling again.

"Come on honey, I'll help you to the bathroom", he told her as he sat up. "You can wear my t-shirt home, and I'll give you one of my hoodies to put over it. I'll keep the sweater and t-shirt and wash them for you. Doc works in a hospital and will know how to get the blood out."

"Thanks", she said happily. "That would be really great."

Once they were both cleaned up and dressed, Brody took her hand and led her out to the common room.

She was surprised at how quiet it was, but she just figured the bikers liked to sleep in.

"Hey Navaho", Brody called. "Is there something wrong? Where is everyone?"

She heard Navaho move closer. "Nah, nothing to be concerned about. You know Ali wasn't feeling the best last night, that's why Cassie stayed with her. She wanted to give Dragon a break, and Steele had to physically pry him away from his girl. Anyway, turns out Ali was in labour. Most of the guys have headed over to the hospital to wait. I'm headed there now, I just wanted to wait and tell you. There's a plate of food for each of you in the oven. I'll see you there in a bit brother", he finished.

Misty heard his footsteps as he moved away, then a door opened and shut.

"Do you want to go to the hospital with me", Brody asked in excitement.

She hated to turn him down again, but she wanted to be honest with him. "I'm sorry, after the accident, I try to stay away from them."

"Shit", he said. "Okay, sorry. Let's eat the breakfast Navaho left for us, then I'll take you home. I'll call you later and let you know what's happening", he promised.

"That would be perfect", she told him in relief.

Brody sat her at a table, then hurried off to get their plates. They ate, and she was surprised at how good everything was. When she heard Brody tapping his foot on the floor, she started to laugh.

"Okay, okay, I'm done", she told him. You can take me home now, so you can go join everyone at the hospital."

"Sorry", he admitted. "But, Ali having her baby is something I want to be there for. I've grown close to her and the brothers over the last little while, so I want to be a part of everything."

"I understand", she told him. "Lets go."

She waited a minute for him to put away their dishes, then he was back, taking her hand and leading her to the bike. It was a quick ride home, then he was parking and leading her up to her apartment.

"I had a great time", she told him.

"Me too", he replied. Then he kissed her, and removed the key from her neck. He unlocked and opened the door, then put it back around her neck. When she heard him move into the apartment she sighed.

"Carly already left for work. I'm going to be here by myself."

"I worry about you being here with her. Will you promise to call me if you need me", he begged.

"I promise", she told him. "I'll be okay though."

He pulled her close and hugged her tight, then his impatience hit again. She laughed when she felt him bouncing on his feet.

"Go", she said. "But call me and tell me everything."

He released her, gave her a quick kiss on her head, then he was gone. She smiled in the direction of her closed door. She was falling hard for him, and as she thought about it for minute, she realized that she already loved him. She pulled the hoodie close and smelled it. He wasn't getting it back.

Chapter Sixteen
Misty

Misty decided to have a long bath after Brody left. She brought her phone in the bathroom with her and set it on the floor beside the tub. She wanted it close by, in case Brody phoned with news about the baby. She ran the water and then stripped and climbed in. She loved baths and had enjoyed them all her life.

She stayed in for a good hour, before the water got too cold, and she was forced to get out. She dried off and got dressed, then started to dry her hair. When she was almost done, the phone rang. She recognized Noah's ring tone and picked it up right away.

"Noah," she happily answered her phone.

"Hey monkey," he replied. "How are you?"

"Good, I haven't had a headache in a while now," she answered.

"Can you see anything yet?"

"No," Misty told him. "Still just shapes and shadows. I really think that's all I'm going to be able to see." She quickly changed the subject.

"How are things over there, you still ducking like I told you?"

He laughed, "yeah monkey, I'm still ducking." Noah was silent for a minute. "This will be my last tour, once this one is finished, I'm coming home for good," he promised.

She immediately started to cry. "That would be a dream come true," she told him honestly. "You have no idea how much I miss you," she told him brokenly.

"What's wrong monkey," he asked in his big brother voice.

"Nothing, just things are hard around here with Carly sometimes."

"You want to explain that," he said angrily.

"I'm not sure," she told him honestly. "With you over there, you have enough on your plate. You can't help me, and it's not that bad, just a couple small things."

"Tell me," he ordered.

"Carly keeps moving things around on me, it really makes it hard. I think she resents looking after me. And, the other night she took me for a walk at the lake, then she left me there in the dark," she told him quietly.

Her brother roared on the other end of the phone, "she what?"

"I'm okay, I called a friend," she assured him.

"And how long did you try to figure it out on your own, before you called the friend," he questioned."

She sighed, he knew her well. "A bit," she admitted.

"Is that all," he asked.

"Yep," she answered quickly.

"So no, but that's all your gonna tell me," he said in frustration. "I need to get home," he growled.

"I met someone," she blurted out.

"I've got another couple minutes. Tell me about him," he ordered.

And for the last few minutes, she told him everything she could about Brody. She told him how he looked, she told him about the club he belonged to, and she told him about their dates. She also told him that Brody was the one to pick her up that night.

Before Noah hung up, he demanded Brody's number, just in case he had said. He also said he would call and talk to Carly as he planned to give her a quick call next anyway. He totally floored her when he admitted he had been thinking of breaking up with her before he left. But, after the accident she had helped a lot, and he changed his mind. He promised her that when he got back, things would change.

There was shouting in the background, and he had to go.

"Love you monkey," he told her.

"Love you too big brother. Stay safe and keep ducking," she replied.

She heard him laugh as he disconnected. She then went to her bedroom and threw herself on the bed. She cried for the next hour solid, like she always did after she hung up with him.

When Brody called again, she was a mess. Ali was still in labour, and not much had happened. He asked what was wrong, and she told him her brother had called. She didn't tell him how they talked about Carly, she only told him how much she missed and worried about him.

So, for the next hour she did the same thing she did with Noah. Only this time, she was telling Brody all about her brother.

Chapter Seventeen
Trike

Trike was thrilled. Things with Misty were getting better and better. He loved spending time with her, and she was becoming increasingly important to him. He was trying to figure out how soon he could get the cabin finished and move her in, but he figured he may have to wait longer.

Ali had finally had the baby. It was a beautiful little girl she and Dragon had named Catherine. Ali was home now, and she wanted Trike to bring Misty over. Misty had been thrilled Ali had the baby, but she wasn't sure about visiting. Apparently, she was worried that with her being blind, she might accidentally hurt the baby. Trike had tried to reassure her, but he needed to take her over there to prove it.

Trike picked her up, and it was only a short ride to the compound, and then the cabins in the back. She climbed off his bike, and he took her hand, leading her to the porch. He had to tell her to relax as the death grip she had on him was cutting off his circulation.

He didn't bother knocking as Ali was expecting him. Trike just pulled open the door and dragged his pretty little blind girl in behind him. Ali immediately squealed when she saw them, and Dragon helped her to her feet, so she could say hi. They both got hugs from Ali, and Trike got a half hug and back slap from Dragon.

Trike led Misty over the couch and sat her down next to Ali. Then he kissed her on the head and told her he'd be outside with Dragon. They left the woman to chat, while the baby was napping, and headed out on the porch.

"Misty doesn't want children," Trike admitted to his brother.

"Because of her disability," Dragon asked.

"Yeah, she thinks she'd kill a baby. She thinks she could accidentally drown it in a bathtub, or it may stick something in its mouth, or pick up something sharp, and she'd never know. I told her lots of blind woman still have kids, but she refuses."

Dragon nodded. "And do you want kids?"

"I want lots of kids," Trike told him. "But, I want her too. Maybe we could adopt some older kids, then they wouldn't need as much looking after. I don't know," Trike sighed. "But, I'm not giving her up. I'll stick by her side, no matter what her decision is."

Dragon pounded him on the back and welcomed him to the club. Another biker struck by the love bug. Trike laughed at that one. The bikers talked for an hour more before deciding the women had had enough girl time. They headed inside, and Trike froze at the sight that greeted him.

Misty was sitting in the corner of the chesterfield, and baby Catherine was curled up in her arms. Misty looked awe struck, and a couple tears rolled down her face. Quickly, Trike pulled out his phone and snapped a picture. Then he moved to the couch and sat down beside her. Immediately, Misty leaned against him, and put her head on his shoulder.

"You okay honey," he questioned.

"I'm great," she told him. He knew she couldn't see the baby, but she was ecstatic she could hold her. When he looked over at Ali, the minx smiled and winked at him. He grinned back, thinking maybe Ali had worked a miracle.

Trike and Misty stayed another hour, then they said their goodbyes, and headed back to the bike. Trike took them for a long ride, hoping it would give Misty sometime to think, before turning the bike toward her apartment.

When they arrived, he walked her up to the door, and helped her inside. Carly wasn't home, so Trike stayed for a few minutes. After a make-out session on the couch, Trike finally had to go. He left with a smile on his face as he looked back at Misty. She had another one of those dazed expressions on her face. His girl liked to make out with him, and he was over the moon about it.

Chapter Eighteen
Misty

Misty was on the couch, reading one of the braille books she had, when the front door opened and Carly came in. She heard something drop, and Carly cursed, then the door slammed shut. Carly's footsteps made it sound like she was stumbling, as she made her way across the living room.

"Are you drunk," Misty asked her.

"Why," Carly almost bellowed. "You gonna call your brother and tattletale on me." Carly hiccuped, then sat down heavily in the armchair beside across from her.

Misty sat in silence, she didn't know what to say. Noah had told her he would talk to Carly, but from the way she was reacting, it sounded like he might have done a little more than talk.

"You have a big mouth," Carly blurted out suddenly. "What, you needed to act like a crybaby and tell your big brother on me. I left you at the lake because of an emergency," she yelled. "You were fine. I even told you how to get home."

Misty heard something crash against the wall behind her, and she cringed. Then, something else crashed against the same wall. She figured Carly had taken off her heels and then thrown them. Suddenly, Carly was in front of her, and Misty leaned back as Carly banged into her knees.

"Your asshole brother called me and gave me shit. He told me I endangered your life by leaving you that night. Noah also said he left with the understanding I would take care of you. He threatened to stop sending me money, and to send it to you instead. He also said we need to have a talk when he gets back," she screamed.

Misty sat there stunned. Her brother had been angry on the phone, she knew that, but apparently he had been angrier than she thought.

"I've been breaking my back, looking after you're sorry ass. I clean for you, I cook for you, and what do I get, shit," she bellowed. "I had everything set up, marriage, kids, a white pocket fence, and you're fucking that up. And he wants to have a talk, well I'm not stupid, I can guess what that fucking means." Carly stopped talking for a minute, and Misty didn't know what to do.

"Pull out your fucking phone," she demanded.

"What," Misty asked in confusion.

"I said, pull out your fucking phone," she screamed right in Misty's face. Misty cringed and pulled her phone out of her back pocket.

"Now, you're fucking up my relationship, I'm gonna fuck up yours. Call that biker you're dating, and break up with him," she ordered.

"No," Misty whispered. "I won't do that."

"You will," Carly screamed again. "If you don't call him, and break up with him right now, I'll arrange for him to have an accident on that fucking bike of his. You want that on your conscience because it will be all your fault. I know a couple guys that would be perfect for the job. They know the club inside and out, and they can make that happen."

"Why," Misty cried. "Why would you do that?"

"Because I fucking hate you. Now I have to suck up to your fucking brother, and figure out a way to fix this. So stop wasting time," she yelled, "and make the call."

No matter what, Misty couldn't let Carly hurt Brody, so she found the button she had programmed Brody's number in, and she hit it. After only two rings, Brody answered.

"Hey honey," he said happily. "I was just thinking about you."

"I can't see you anymore," Misty blurted out while she cried.

"Come again," Brody said quietly.

"I'm sorry I wasted your time," she cried. "I've just decided that I don't want to be with a biker. I don't like bikers," she told him. "I don't like your friends, and I don't want to do this anymore." She stopped talking, and Brody was silent on the other end of the phone.

"This is what you want," he asked.

"Yes," she sobbed. "Bye Brody," she whispered as she hung up the phone. Then she hugged her phone to her chest, and sobbed, as she ran to her bedroom. Even after slamming the door, she could hear Carly laughing.

Chapter Nineteen
Trike

"Fuck," Trike yelled, as he shoved his phone back in his back pocket. He stood from the chair he was sitting in, and lifted it, then threw it with everything he had at the wall. It crashed and splintered into hundreds of tiny pieces. Every brother in the common room stopped what they were doing, to look at him. He roared in frustration, then hung his head. Steele was beside him in a second, thumping him on the back.

"Did that help brother," Steele questioned. All Trike could do, was shake his head.

"Sit," he ordered, as he pulled out another chair for Trike. More chairs scraped as they dragged them across the floor. Trike looked up to find Steele,

Navaho, Dagger, Dragon and Preacher surrounding him. They were all watching him.

"Tell us," Preacher ordered.

Trike slumped in his chair. "She told me she doesn't want to see me anymore," he admitted.

"Did she tell you why", Dagger asked.

"She said she doesn't like bikers, and she doesn't like my friends," he told them.

Dragon snorted. "She loved us, and she's head over heals for you."

"I know," Trike said. "I don't believe anything she said. She was in tears the whole time, and when she said goodbye, it sounded like it was breaking her to say it," he told them.

She had sounded upset on the phone, and if she didn't want to be with him anymore, she wouldn't have sounded like that. That meant only one thing, someone was making her say that.

"I think her roommate Carly forced her to make that call," he admitted. "The girls a wackjob, and I wouldn't put it past her to pull something like this."

"So she's holding something over her head," Steele said. "We just have to figure out what it is and make it go away."

"The girls blind," Trike said, "she's at Carly's mercy in that apartment. Carly makes everything difficult for Misty too."

"Fuck," Navaho said. "So we do some reconnaissance and try to figure out what the hell the girls blackmailing her with. After meeting her, my bet is that it involves you or her brother. How long do we give her, before we storm the castle and slay the dragon," he asked.

"A week," Preacher answered. "Long enough to figure stuff out and make Carly think we believe Misty. Maybe then, she'll let her guard down, and we'll get lucky. I don't want to leave it longer than that because I don't want to put your girl at risk."

All the brothers nodded their head in agreement. Preacher clapped Trike on the back.

"Get that cabin finished," he ordered. "You may need it." Then Preacher stood and left the room.

"I'm free the next couple days," Dagger said. "I'll help with the cabin."

"I can put in a bit of time," Dragon said. "But I have a newborn at home, and a beautiful wife. No offence, but I'd rather spend time with them." All the brothers laughed, then ribbed him a bit.

With the mood lifted, Trike felt better. They made plans and decided they would put a man on Carly at all times. They'd also dig deeper into her background, and try to pull her cell phone records, and bank records. It was time to put this bitch in her place, and help Misty.

"Do we use our contacts, and try to reach the brother," Steele asked.

"No," Trike immediately said. "He's fighting in Afghanistan and doesn't need the added worry. If something goes down he needs to know, we'll make the call then. According to Misty, it's his last tour, and after this he'll be home for good. It may only be another month before that happens, let's let the man finish his tour in peace, and take care of this ourselves," Trike told his brothers.

Again, the brothers agreed. Trike felt better, knowing he had his brothers support. One week was all he was giving this, after that week, he would get his girl, and he would explain to her what being his meant.

Chapter Twenty
Misty

Misty was miserable. It had been two days since Carly forced her to break up with Brody, and she missed him immensely. Somehow, in a short amount of time, he had become an important part of her life. He was a caring, considerate and thoughtful man. He also made her laugh, and she missed riding on the back of his bike.

A tear ran down her cheek as she thought about him again. Misty had cried so much in the last two days; it surprised her she had any tears left. She was in the living room now, but whenever Carly was home, Misty would try to stay in her room. Things were tense between the two of them.

Misty heard a key in the lock, and jumped to her feet, but the door opened before she could get around the couch.

"Running away," Carly taunted as she walked in. Misty turned, but was surprised when she heard a second set of footprints enter as well. She knew immediately that it was a man because the steps were heavier. She held the back of the couch and leaned slightly against it.

"So this is the blind girl," the man asked.

"Yep," Carly agreed. "The pain in my ass."

"She's a pretty little thing," he said, as his footsteps got closer.

She cringed, when she felt a finger run down the side of her face, and down her throat. He stopped just shy of her breast, and she reached up and grabbed his hand to stop it from going lower. She shoved it away, and leaned back, trying to put some distance between them.

"Don't touch me," she said angrily. She heard him laugh, and felt his breath on her cheek, as he moved closer once more.

"I heard you're a single lady now. My best friend would love you. I think maybe we need to set up a date between you two," he told her. "He likes shy, quiet girls like you, it brings out the animal in him."

Misty pushed him as hard as she could, then hurried past him and moved towards the hall. She heard Carly tell him to wait outside, but she kept walking. She had just reached her room when Carly caught up with her.

"Is that the guy you're cheating on my brother with," Misty asked her.

"I'm flirting," Carly sneered. "And last time I checked, that's not cheating. Besides, he's good looking, he really likes me, and he's around all the time, not like your brother."

Misty wasn't in the mood to fight, so she sighed and asked, "what do you want Carly?"

"I'm headed out with my friend, then I'll be back to pack. I'll be gone for three days, so you'll be on your own," she said.

"Where are you going," Misty asked.

"It's none of your business, but maybe when I get back, we can set up that double date."

"I'm not going out with him." Misty said angrily.

"You don't have to go out with him," Carly huffed. "We can invite them over here, and order take out. It could be a romantic evening in."

"No," Misty yelled. "That's not happening."

"Well," Carly sighed. "Then your life's gonna be pretty lonely. Anyway, I'll be back soon, and I'll have my friend with me. He's gonna help me pack, then I'll be off."

As Carly turned and walked away, Misty thought of something else.

"What's your friend name." she asked.

"None of your fucking business," Carly yelled over her shoulder as she stomped through the living room. Then Misty heard the front door slam as she left.

It thrilled her she would be Carly free for the next couple of days, but she knew it would be boring. She couldn't even call Ali since breaking up with Brody meant she broke up with her too. And she was curious why Carly wouldn't tell her what her friends name was. For some reason, she thought that might be important.

Chapter Twenty One
Trike

Trike was pacing Dragon's porch. He missed his girl, and it had only been two days, how was he supposed to wait five more. He had a new prospect, Shadow, watching the building. Carly had come and gone several times, but they never saw Misty. Yesterday, Shadow reported that Carly had brought a man with her twice. They now had the prospect carry a camera, and they hoped to get a picture of the man.

Carly never saw Shadow, but no one ever did. He was an ex-military man, and his job had been to collect enemy Intel. He was in and out of places like a ghost. Because of that, the prospect was useful, and he loved utilizing his skill set.

"You're gonna wear a hole through my fucking porch," Dragon growled at him, as he held a sleeping Catherine on his shoulder. "If Ali sees it, she'll put me in the doghouse which means I put you in the lake. Don't you have a cabin to work on or something?"

"It's done, with all the help I've gotten lately, it went faster than I expected. Cassie even helped me pick out furniture, it was all delivered this morning. Maybe I should go relieve Shadow. He's been there a while and may need a break," he decided.

"Sit the fuck down brother and settle. If Carly sees you, she'll either start something, or take it out on your girl. You got to be smart about this. Stick with the plan, it's a couple days more, that's all," Dragon told him.

Trike sat, but did so reluctantly. "I need to know she's okay," he sighed. "She sounded awful on the phone, and it kills me to think of her hurting like that."

Dragon turned in his chair and yelled for Ali through the window. In seconds Ali came outside, smiling when she saw her husband with their tiny daughter.

"You want me to take her," she asked him, as she leaned over and gave him a quick kiss.

"No," he answered, pulling Catherine closer to his chest. "I want you to call Misty and get a feel for what's going on with her. Trike's worried about his girl, so I need you to find out what you can."

Ali nodded and pulled out her phone. She sat on the porch steps as it rang. Trike stood quickly, offering his chair, but Ali waved him off. He waited patiently, listening to Ali's side of the conversation.

"Misty it's Ali, I wondered if you wanted to do lunch today," Trike heard her ask.

"Oh I'm so sorry, I didn't hear. I thought you liked him, you even told me you were falling for him." Trike waited with bated breath for Ali to speak again.

"But you knew he was a biker when you met him, and you never had a problem with it before. You even told me how much you love riding on the back of his bike." Trike smiled, Ali was good at pushing. She was silent for a while as she listened, then she frowned.

"What could be going on, that would make it a bad time to date right now." Again there was a pause before Ali questioned her again. "You need to look after yourself, you can't be thinking about what's easier for others. Do you still care about him," Ali asked. Trike stared at Ali in anticipation.

"Then you need to work this out." Ali frowned then ended the call. "She gave me the brush off and hung up," she sighed.

Ali turned her full attention on Trike. "Misty's miserable. She said things are difficult for her right now, and she needs to be by herself. She was stumbling over her answers and kept saying different things. Misty wouldn't get into the reasons. But, she still cares about you, and was crying at the end. She repeated that she couldn't see you right now right, and she then hung up."

Trike smiled big. "She still wants me," he said as he stood. "Fuck a week, she's got one more day to come to her senses, before I get her," he growled.

Chapter Twenty Two
Misty

Misty cried for an hour after hanging up on Ali. She liked the girl, and she hated lying to her, but she couldn't see her anymore either. She didn't expect to hear from any of them again, and Ali's call had surprised her.

Misty wished her life was different. She wanted her brother to come home and help her. She had no life anymore. She couldn't work, so she sat in her room all day, she barely went outside, and she didn't talk to anyone. It was like she didn't exist anymore.

She heard a lot of banging last night, and she knew Carly was packing. The man had been with her, and he terrified Misty, so she had hid in her room. The apartment was deathly quiet this morning, so she knew Carly had left, like she said she would. Misty was over the moon, this meant she had two days to herself.

Dragging herself out of bed, she headed for the bathroom and had a quick shower. Then she made her way to the kitchen and poured up a bowl of dry cereal. She craved bacon and eggs, but there was no way she could cook that by herself. She sat at the counter and ate with her fingers. A spoon was tricky when she couldn't see. When she was done, she tossed the bowl in the sink.

Sitting at the counter, she contemplated her life. She couldn't see, and it was clear that her sight wasn't coming back. That meant, her photography business was something she could never do again. She was living with Carly and she hated it. Carly was putting her life in danger, and now she was threatening her. Not only that, but she did not understand who the man was that Carly had brought around, and he terrified her.

Misty had to do something. She pulled her cell out of her pocket and dialled her brother. He didn't answer, but she explained as fast as she could about Carly's threats against Brody, about how she had forced her to break up with him, and about the man and his threats. She kept it as short as she could, knowing her brother would call her as soon as he got the message.

Next, she tried to figure out what to do about Brody. She loved him; she knew it without a doubt, and she wanted to be with him. He was a biker, and he had the whole club behind him, surely he could take on Carly. The threat to his bike worried her, but she could warn him about that. She picked her phone back up and called him, happy that he answered on the first ring.

"You gonna tell me what threat she used to get you to break up with me," he asked without even saying hello. She sighed, not surprised Brody hadn't believed a word she said.

"Carly told me she knew some people who could tamper with your bike," she admitted. "I didn't want you hurt. I'm so sorry," she said as she cried.

"I think you need to tell me everything that's been going on," he ordered.

"Okay," she whispered through her tears. "Just let me go sit in the living room, then I'll tell you it all."

She headed in that direction, and put her hand out, expecting it to hit the couch, but it didn't. She flailed for a minute, trying to catch herself, but it was no use, she fell forward and screamed as she went threw the glass coffee table.

Her arm was out, so that hit first, and she could feel the glass tearing it up. Then her side hit, and she felt more glass cut into her skin. When she landed she fell on all the rest of the broken glass. She kept screaming, as the glass shards continued to cut into her, until she passed out.

Chapter Twenty Three
Trike

Trike listened in horror, as he heard Misty scream, then he heard the never ending sound of breaking glass. His heart stopped, as she screamed for a minute longer, then ceased altogether. He roared her name, over and over, but she never answered.

Trike heard pounding feet, and then Steele and Dragon were beside him. He had just left Dragon's cabin, so they both must have heard him. He ignored them as he kept calling out for her.

Suddenly, Steele was roaring into his phone. Trike heard him order Shadow, the prospect that was sitting outside the apartment, to go inside and get to Misty.

Then Dragon was pounding him on the back to get his attention.

"Explain," he ordered.

Trike took a deep breath and told his brothers about the scream and the breaking glass. Without missing a beat, Steele grabbed onto him, and dragged him toward his truck, while Dragon called the doctor and told him to get to the clubhouse with his medical supplies.

While running to the truck, Trike kept the phone to his ear, begging his pretty little blind girl to answer. All he got was silence, until a crash sounded, and then he heard Shadow cursing. All of them reached the truck, and jumped in, as Steele tore off. Then he heard Shadow's heavy boots on the floor, as he pounded through the apartment.

It felt like hours before Steele's phone rang. Steele grabbed it and threw it to Dragon as he was too busy tearing through town. He heard Dragon answer, then a minute later he hung up. He swore, then turned back to face Trike.

"Brother," he said. "It's bad. Looks like your girl somehow fell through a glass coffee table. Shadow's lifted her out of the mess, but she's covered in cuts, and some have glass sticking out. He's got her wrapped in towels, where he can, but there's quite a bit of blood."

"Just get me to her," Trike told them. He was barely holding it together, but he knew he had to be strong for her.

When they arrived, and pulled up into the front of the building, Trike was out before the truck even stopped. He pulled open the front door that was hanging at an odd angle, curtesy of Shadow, and pounded up the stairs. When he reached the apartment and stepped inside, he froze, looking at the scene in horror.

The coffee table was obviously smashed, and it lay in the middle of the floor. Blood and glass surrounded it. His eyes darted around the room, and he noticed the couch pushed against the back wall. He ignored that and turned to find Shadow. The brother was kneeling on the floor in front of the kitchen counter, and Misty lay beside him.

Trike hurried over and knelt down beside Shadow. Misty was covered in blood and was deathly pale. She had cuts on the whole right side of her body. He looked at her, not knowing where to touch her, as glass protruded from several places. Shadow placed his hand on his arm.

"Come over to this side," he instructed. "She doesn't have any injuries over here. That's how I picked her up. Just cradle her against your side and make sure you don't hit any of the glass.

Trike did as they told him, carefully lifting her, and heading for the door. Steele and Dragon were beside him, and they both wore menacing expressions. Dragon ordered Shadow to fix Misty's apartment door before he left, seeing as the prospect had broken down that one as well. Shadow nodded, and watched, as they hurried down the stairs and got into the truck.

Again Steele tore through the town, and Trike prayed that doc could help her. He loved her, and he wasn't ready to lose her yet.

Chapter Twenty Four
Trike

Trike carried Misty through the common room and headed down the hall to his room. All the brothers stood to the side and looked on angrily. They all took unkindly to violence against women, but this was also against someone with a disability.

Not only that, but they would have to figure out how to deal with another woman. They couldn't just take her out to the shed, chain her up, and light her up with the blowtorch. They would have to get creative with this one.

Trike reached his room and was glad to see the doc was already there. He had covered the bed in a ton of towels, and instructed Trike to lay her, so she was tipped her up on her good side. Trike crossed the room and gently laid her on her left side. This meant she was facing them.

The doc then explained that he wanted to give her a shot containing a sedative. He explained that removing the glass and stitching her up would be extremely painful, and he didn't want her waking up in the middle. When he was done with the shot, he took out a pair of scissors and cut her clothes off. Trike immediately shut the door on his brothers, blocking out all their concerned faces.

It took five minutes to get her down to her underwear, and Trike thought she looked worse with the clothes off. Doc thoroughly checked her over and decided which spots needed the most attention. The first was a huge piece of glass that was protruding from her side. Doc carefully removed it and announced that nothing major was hit. He stitched that one up and moved on to the next one.

Four hours later, the glass was removed, and Misty was all stitched up. Trike had counted one hundred and three pieces of glass they removed. Some were no bigger than a sliver while others were the size of a pencil. Doc said the table must have been cheap to shatter that badly, but it was a good thing. If the glass shards had been any bigger, Misty might not have made it.

As it was, it badly damaged Misty's arm, as it had taken the brunt of the fall. She would heal, but her arm would need to be constantly checked, and would probably scar. The doc had wrapped the entire thing and has placed it in a sling. It would be painful for a long time, and she would have to be careful of all the stitches.

Her thigh also suffered a deep cut, but doc said she could walk on it. The last cut, was a deep one across her forehead. Doc stitched it up and then placed gauze over it. She was lucky her face wasn't cut up more.

Doc gave her two more shots. One contained pain medicine, and the other was an antibiotic. He explained that her biggest battle now would be to fight off any infection. The cuts would have to be checked twice a day, and an ointment would have to be applied. Also, he explained that she would be weak from the blood loss. It wasn't enough that he needed to give her a transfusion, but it was enough to affect her.

It broke Trike's heart to see his girl like this. Doc helped place one of his shirts over her head while

Trike held her, then he removed all the bloodied towels. It surprised Trike to see a sheet of plastic lay underneath them all. Once that was removed too, his bed was spotless.

Doc moved to the door and explained that he would stay in Dragon's old room for the next couple days. Trike thanked him, then moved aside as Preacher, Steele, Dragon, Navaho and Dagger pushed inside. They surrounded the bed and stared down at Misty. Trike stood by and watched, as each brother kissed her cheek, then left his room. He knew without asking that his brothers had just declared Misty one of their own.

Chapter Twenty Five
Trike

Trike stayed with Misty while she slept. He got as close to her as possible, but made sure not to touch her. He watched her chest rise and fall, and held her hand, just happy that she was gonna be okay. It was the middle of the day, and Trike was starving, so he got up. He rolled towels up, and placed them behind and in front of her, so she would stay on her side.

Trike headed to the common room. As soon as he sat beside Steele, Navaho was there, placing a sandwich in front of him. He nodded his thanks, then dug in. One by one, Dragon, Dagger and Navaho joined them. The brothers waited patiently, and drank their beers, as they waited for him to finish.

Finally done, he pushed the plate away, and told them the extent of her injuries. They listened, then Steele spoke up.

"We keep her in your room a couple days, then we move her to your cabin. There's lots of help here, and you may need it. Once you get to the cabin, you'll be a bit more isolated. How long do you figure she'll sleep for," he questioned?

"Doc said she'd be out for hours. He gave her a heavy sedative and said sleeps the best thing for her right now."

"Right," Steele said. "So I say we take a couple trucks, and head to the apartment. I think it's time to move her out. Not only that, but with the girlfriend away, I think we ought to move the brothers shit out too. If I were him, I'd want to know someone here had my back. There's no telling what the girlfriend could pull after this."

Trike nodded in agreement, then looked up as the front door opened. Shadow moved across the room and sat at the only free chair left. He reached in his pocket, and pulled out a cell, pushing it across the table.

"This is your girls. I cleaned it as best I could. It's gone off twice, but I didn't think it was my place to answer." He then pushed two keys across the table. "I fixed the door, but it was trashed, apparently I was too rough with it," he smirked.

The brothers snorted, and it eased the tension. "These are the only two keys. I didn't give one to the landlord, so we need to get over there pronto. He wasn't too happy about being locked out of one of his apartments. I told him we'd get him one by the end of the day." Shadow paused until he had all the brothers attention.

"They pushed the couch up against the far wall, and the coffee table was in a direct line from the kitchen. There is no way in hell that wasn't moved intentionally. My guess is that the girlfriend was hoping your girl would be stuck there for a while. This could have been really bad," he stated.

Trike nodded, "and that's all I can think about," he told them.

Dragon pounded him on the back. "She's one of us now, we got her covered." He pulled out his cell and called doc, asking him to sit with Misty for a while.

Then they loaded up into three trucks and headed back to the apartment.

The landlord cornered them before they even got inside. Navaho smoothed things over with him, and then explained they were moving the girls out, and would turn in the key once they were done.

Trike raised his eyebrow in question, but Navaho just smirked. "No idea who's stuff is who's, so I figure we load it all up. We can store it at the compound for now."

All the brothers laughed and pounded Navaho on the back. Then they sent Shadow with Dagger to rent a U-Haul. Biker vengeance was a bitch, and this was just the beginning.

Chapter Twenty Six
Trike

Trike, Steele, Navaho and Dragon entered the apartment together. Trike couldn't take his eyes off the broken coffee table, and all the surrounding blood. He could still picture his pretty little blind girl, laying there unconscious.

Dragon slapped him on the back. "We got a lot to do brother, so you can get back to your girl. We leave this mess here and concentrate on all the other rooms. You start on your girl's room, and I'll start on the bitches."

Trike nodded and headed down the hall. When he pushed open the door, he realized this would be a piece of cake. Someone covered the entire far wall of her room with unopened boxes, his girl hadn't even unpacked. He moved to the boxes and glanced at them.

One in particular caught his attention though. Someone labeled it photography. He pulled it out, and opened it up. Several very expensive cameras sat inside, along with a box of jump drives. He wondered if this was what Misty had done before the accident. He packed it back up and put it aside. His poor girl had lost a lot more than her sight.

Trike moved on, and used the garbage bags he had brought, to empty her closet. He didn't touch her dresser as he figured he'd just pick the whole thing up and carry it out. He was almost done, and headed to the bathroom, when his phone rang. When he glanced down, the caller was unknown. Trike accepted the call.

"Trike," he said in agitation, as he tried to keep shoving things in bags.

"Tell me you know where my sister is," a voice on the other end demanded.

"Shit," Trike said.

"What do you know, because I got a phone call from Misty the other day, that was upsetting? Now it's two days later, and I can't reach her."

"You want the sugar coated version, or you want the facts," Trike asked him.

"Fuck," Noah swore. "Just tell me."

Trike sighed then ran through what had happened in the apartment, and how they suspected Carly of moving things on purpose. He then ran through Misty's injuries. Noah was furious and concerned. Trike made sure her brother knew a doctor was looking after her, and she had the whole club behind her. That seemed to ease Noah's mind.

They talked for a bit more about Carly, then Trike wanted to know if Noah had any feelings for her. He didn't want to upset the brother, but he explained that there would be consequences. He then told him what they were doing, and Noah was all for it. As far as her brother was concerned, there was no relationship any longer, and they could do what they wanted.

The conversation ended with Noah explaining that he had started the paperwork to get discharged. Apparently, his contract was up, and he was only there to finish this last tour. He hoped to be home within a week or two. Trike promised to keep him up to date, and to make sure Misty was well taken care of. When they hung up, they had formed a friendship, and Trike was glad Noah had phoned.

About an hour later, the entire apartment, minus the living room, was packed up. Navaho spoke to the landlord and told him they were finished, and that in two weeks he was free to rent it out. They figured that was plenty of time for Carly to return and find the locks changed, and everything she owned gone.

Trike and his brothers drove back to the compound, and emptied what they assumed was Carly's belongings, into an empty storage bay. The rest, minus Misty's clothes and bathroom supplies, went into the spare bedroom of Trike's cabin.

Trike smiled as he headed back to his room in the compound. Misty was all moved in, and she didn't even know it. She was his now, and he'd do anything to protect her and make her happy. She now had a huge family that had just adopted her, and Trike couldn't wait to tell her. Her life would be better from now on.

Chapter Twenty Seven
Misty

Misty woke, unsure of where she was. The bed felt different, and it smelled like Brody. She kept her eyes shut as she turned and smelled his pillow.

"Are you smelling my bed," she heard a laughing Brody ask.

"Yes," she admitted. "It smells like you."

Misty felt the bed dip and then a light kiss was placed on her cheek. She tried moving, to get closer, but pain shot through the entire right side of her body. She cried out as tears rolled down her face.

"Easy," Brody said as he wiped at them with his finger. "You're pretty cut up from your little swan dive through the coffee table."

"The couch wasn't there," Misty whispered,. "I reached for it, but it wasn't there. I was falling, but there was nothing to grab," she told him.

Misty felt his hands on both her cheeks, and his lips on her head. "Oh honey," he said. "I think we need to get pain meds into you again. Are you going to open your eyes, pretty girl? I know you can't see either way, but I like looking at them," he teased as he tweaked her nose.

She opened her eyes and then gasped in shock. Brody was sitting in front of her, and she could make out his large frame. He was still blurry, but she could see his long blonde hair and muscular build. She couldn't see his face clearly, and she couldn't see his clothing, but she knew he was wearing a black shirt and jeans. She began to sob hysterically.

Brody moved to lie on the bed beside her. He tried to pull her closer, and as much as it hurt, she let him.

"You'll be okay Misty mine, I'll make sure. And you never have to go back there, from now on you stay with me," he ordered in her ear.

She pulled away slightly so she could look at him again. Carefully, she raised her hand, and touched his cheek. Then she moved it up and ran her fingers through his hair. The she took his hand and kissed the palm.

"Fuck," she heard Brody swear. "Misty mine, can you see me?"

"Sort of," she told him. "It's not clear, but I can see your shape more clearly. I can see your blonde hair, and I know you're wearing jeans and a black t-shirt. I can see the colour. But I can't see very clearly," she admitted. "I can't see your eyes, and I don't know if you have any marks or scars."

She moved to place her hand on his arm. "I can see black ink, but it all blurs together."

He kissed her again. "The fall," he told her. "You hit your head hard, and you have a fair sized lump and cut on your forehead. Maybe that helped your vision somehow," he said. "That is how you lost it in the first place."

She thought about it and agreed. She tried to move again, and whimpered, the pain was terrible.

"Okay, let's get that pain medicine into you. I can help you sit up, and you can take it with some food. Doc said it's strong, so you may want something in your stomach first. Navaho has french toast warming in the oven for you, if you're interested," he told her.

"God yes," she said. "That sounds perfect." She couldn't move her arm though and wasn't sure why.

"Your arm suffered the worst of the glass," he explained. "It's bandaged entirely, and Doc put it in a sling so you wouldn't move it. You have a shit ton of stitches, and it's probably gonna scar," he told her sympathetically.

"I can't go back there," she told him.

"Hell no," he declared. "You're staying here with me, where I can protect you. You're mine now, and I'm taking that extremely seriously. Things are gonna look up for you honey, and I'll make sure of that."

She heard every word, but could only concentrate on one. "Yours," she told him.

"Damn straight," he told her. Then he kissed her, and it last a long time, so long she forgot all about the french toast.

Chapter Twenty Eight
Trike

Trike was careful with Misty. She had a lot of stitches, and he wanted none to pull. He was glad to see her eat all the French toast Navaho had brought her and take all the meds doc had left for her. Both would help her heal quickly. She got tired of laying in bed on her side though, so Trike helped her up.

She got tearful when she saw her clothes, stacked neatly in his small closet. Trike just told her to get used to it, and she giggled at his possessiveness. She didn't seem to mind that about him, though, and that made things easier.

A few minutes later, they were in the common room, and surrounded by his brothers. They were all concerned about her and treated her like glass. She seemed a bit overwhelmed, but happy. Misty didn't want to mention her eyesight as she was afraid it was only temporary. She still couldn't see everything either, so Trike figured he'd get doc to look at her, when he came to change the bandages.

Preacher's phone rang then, and everyone stopped talking to look at him. He opened it and listened for a minute, then snapped it closed.

"Shadow's on the gate. He said our two favourite detectives are back," he explained.

With a sigh, Trike turned to the doors just as the detectives walked in. He got Misty comfortable at one of the tables, then went over to shake hands with the detectives.

"What can we do for you today," Preacher asked.

"We have a kidnaping complaint, and a theft to look into," one detective explained.

"Who the hells kidnapped," Steele asked.

"Misty Bradley," the detective replied.

"I'm right here," Misty said, waving from the table she was sitting at.

The detectives instantly headed towards her, then froze when they got close. "What happened to you," one of them asked.

"I fell through a glass coffee table," she said shrugging. "Who said someone kidnapped me," she asked.

"Your roommate Carly. She came to the police station this morning saying someone had kidnapped you. The landlord said bikers took you out, and you were unconscious and covered in blood. Then they came back later and emptied the apartment. Carly filed charges against you all," he explained.

Misty stood up, and Trike rushed to her side to support her.

"First," she said. "I got this way because Carly moved the furniture around. I'm blind, and couldn't see things weren't where they should be. Second, I was on the phone with Brody and he rushed over to help me. Third, all these bikers helped move me out, seeing as I wasn't ever going back there. And, seeing as I was in no condition to tell them who's stuff was who's, they took it all. Last, the apartments in my brothers name, and he approved of the move," she said as she glared at the detectives.

Both of the detectives laughed, and that just caused Misty to glare harder.

"You know," one of them said. "I'm gonna get myself assigned to this club permanently. This job is boring as hell, but since I've been dealing with all you, I've looked forward to going to work. Kidnappings, bombs, motorcycle chases and shootouts, best job ever," he declared.

Preacher smirked at the detective, "glad we could help."

"We'll need to confirm with the brother," the detective said. "Then everything should be fine."

"My brothers a marine stationed in Afghanistan," Misty explained. "I'm hoping he'll be home in a couple weeks."

"Oh, well we can just put this case on hold until we hear from him, no rush. But Carly's pissed and looking for payback. Watch your backs around her. We can't turn around and charge her with anything, seeing as it's not illegal to move furniture, and she wasn't home at the time of the accident."

Preacher nodded in understanding, then turned and escorted the detectives to the door.

"If you need us for anything, call us," the detective said. "We'll hold Carly off until we speak to the brother and let her know we can't do anything until then." Then they shook hands with Preacher and left.

"Fucking detectives," Preacher growled, and all the brothers laughed.

Chapter Twenty Nine
Misty

Misty was frustrated. It was the day after the detectives came, and she was in a lot of pain. She was taking the pain pills, but her arm was extremely tender. Any movement, set off a shot of fire through it. She was grateful for the sling she was wearing.

Her sight hadn't changed any more either. She was still seeing a bit better, and she could make out colours, but the later it got in the day, the worse it became. Doc said, that by the end of the day, her eyes were getting tired, and that was to be expected. He was very hopeful that given time, it would get better and better.

Brody was a lifesaver. He took her for walks; he took her to the common room to eat, and he entertained her with stories of the bikers. She also got introduced to Cassie, and they hit it off. Cassie helped her get cleaned up and even helped her wash her hair. It made Misty feel one hundred percent better.

Noah had called that morning too, and Misty had broke down sobbing. Luckily, Trike had been with her. She explained to Noah what had happened, and Noah was furious. He wanted to be there. He promised though, that as soon as he got home, he would deal with Carly. The paperwork was being pushed through, and he hoped it wouldn't be too much longer.

After that draining phone call, Cassie and Ali showed up with baby Catherine, and declared it to be a girl's day. They listened to music, they laughed, and they gave Misty a makeover. They also went through her clothes, and picked out all her yoga pants and tees, so she would be comfortable while she healed. After pizza and a tub of ice cream, the girls left, but they promised to be back soon. It thrilled Misty, she'd never had friends like them before.

Then, her evening was broken up by Carly coming to the front gate and screaming. Trike wanted to deal with it, but Misty wanted to stand up for herself. When they approached the gate, surrounded by Dragon, Steele, Dagger, Navaho, Preacher and Shadow, it gave Misty the courage she needed.

Carly didn't seem surprised at all by her injuries and didn't even ask about them. She yelled and accusing them of stealing her stuff. Misty tried to explain that when she was feeling better, she'd go through everything, and return what was hers. Carly refused to listen to reason, yelling she had been kicked out of her own apartment too, and had nowhere to stay.

Misty calmly mentioned that maybe she could stay with the man she was with the other night. That probably wasn't the smartest thing to say, because Carly ran at the gates, and pounded on them. The bikers only looked on in amusement. But then they full out laughed, when she tried to climb the gate, in her high-heeled shoes and tiny dress.

That was when a car pulled up, and the detectives got out. They stood there looking up at her, and laughing with the bikers, as Carly got nowhere. Then one detective moved towards the fence.

"Steele," he said, while still laughing. "Appreciate the call. Again, best job ever." Then the two detectives moved to Carly and physically pulled her off the fence. She fought and squirmed, and got free, only to land in a puddle on the ground.

She looked up and then fake tears rolled down her face. One detective finally had enough and told her to knock it off. Immediately, the tears stopped, and she cursed at them. One detective dragged her off, while the other shook his head, and said his goodbyes. They pulled away with Carly in the backseat.

"What do we do with her car," Dagger asked.

"Let's have it towed," Shadow declared. Misty nodded her head in complete agreement. Payback was a bitch, but Misty learned it also a lot of fun.

Chapter Thirty
Trike

Trike was sitting at the bar in the common room, having a beer with Dagger. He was having a shitty day, so he decided a drink was in order, while Misty had a nap. She had woken up this morning in a lot of pain. Doc was still staying here, so Trike had run down the hall to get him.

Doc had unwrapped the bandages and checked out the many cuts. Unfortunately, one had gotten an infection. Doc assured Misty and him, that sometimes this happened, and they had done nothing to cause it. He gave her a strong shot of antibiotics, and another shot of pain mess, and it had knocked her out.

Trike was worried about her. The injuries were healing slowly, and he knew it was getting to her. Her sight was still the same too, and he had called her eye specialist, and gotten her an appointment for two days from now. He wanted to know exactly what was happening with her eyes.

Trike was also thwarting calls from Carly. The girl was pissed, and he had confiscated Misty's phone, because she was calling every couple hours. They were just nasty threats, but Trike didn't want Misty bothered by them.

He looked up as Ali and Cassie walked into the room. As they looked to be headed right for him, he turned on his chair. Ali spoke first.

"Trike, can you take us down to the dentist office for a second? The guys are watching Catherine, and I've got a sore tooth," she whined.

Trike sighed, but nodded in agreement. "My trucks parked outside," Cassie said, as she threw him the keys.

They headed out, and it only took minutes to reach the dentist office. The girls were unnaturally quiet on the way over, so he figured Ali's tooth must have been bad. He climbed out of the truck and held the door open as the girl's stepped inside.

Then all hell broke loose as the girls yelled for the manager. Trike did not understand what was going on, but he tried to calm them both down. A man came rushing out the back, demanding to know what was going on.

Trike could only stare as Cassie stepped forward. "You have a receptionist working here by the name of Carly," she demanded.

Trike cursed, as the man nodded. "I do, what seems to be the problem."

"Your receptionist hit on both our husbands, and we want to have a word with her. This is a place of business, and I don't appreciate you letting your employees treat it like a brothel. Our husbands refuse to come back, and we want her fired," she demanded.

The manager looked flustered. "I'm so sorry," he apologized. "I expect my employees to act professionally, I'll deal with her right away," he promised.

"If she isn't fired by the end of today, you'll lose all our business," Ali threatened. "And we know many people in this town, we'll make sure they're aware of what happened here."

The man was nearly begging the girls now, and Trike couldn't hide his smile. "I guarantee, she will be gone long before then," he stammered.

Both girls turned on their heels and headed for the door, Trike had to hurry over, so he could open it for them. As they marched back to the truck, Trike laughed.

"You girls are viscous," he told them. "I think the brothers could learn some things from you."

"She's messing with your girl," Cassie said. Then she grabbed his arm and stopped him as he reached the truck. "You saved my life, and I'll never be able to repay you. If I can even help you a little, I will. Besides, I like your girl, she belongs with you," she said.

Trike leaned over and kissed her head. "Best damn thing I ever did, was join this club," he stated. "Best damn thing." Then he got the girls in and settled and turned the truck towards the compound. He drove them home, with a huge ass smile on his face.

"Fucking women," he laughed.

Chapter Thirty One
Misty

Misty was nervous. Today, Brody was taking her to the eye specialist. Her sight had improved a bit over the last couple days, but not like it had that first day. She still couldn't see things clearly, but the colours and shapes were getting better.

Her arm was still painful, but the infection that had flared up two days ago, was going down. Doc was keeping a close eye on it and cleaning it twice a day. He had also insisted on her taking pain medication, which she wasn't thrilled about. She had three more days before the stitches came out.

This afternoon, Brody had taken her outside to eat lunch. He had made sandwiches, and they had sat on a blanket under a tree, while they ate. Brody knew she was nervous about what the eye specialist would say, so he had been trying to get her to relax. It was just what she needed, and she enjoyed her time with him a lot. They kissed, but with her arm so messed up, it didn't go as far as she would have liked.

Reluctantly, they packed up and headed to Brody's room, so Misty could clean up a bit before they left. Brody opened the door to his room and stopped so fast, Misty hit his back.

"Fucking bikers," he grumbled. "I was expecting something, but this?"

Misty pushed past him and entered. The first thing she noticed was the floor. Instead of the hard, cold wood, the floor was soft and fluffy. She kicked off her flip flops and walked around on it. She could make out a variety of colours, but she didn't know what it was. Misty moved to the bed, and sat down, gasping when she found it too was soft and cozy.

"What is it," she asked Brody, as group of bikers appeared at the door.

"Well darling," she heard Steele say. "You know the story of what happens to our rooms when we find our girl," he asked. She nodded her head yes.

"You can't see, so it wouldn't make a difference if we changed the colour of some things. So," he continued, "we covered the floor in fun fur, and the quilt on the bed, is made of a soft jersey material. To piss Trike off, it's all in a rainbow pattern," he declared.

Misty laughed, and all the bikers joined in, except for Brody. She couldn't see him well, but she knew he was glaring at them all.

"Okay fuckers, everyone out," he grumbled. "You got your laugh, now I have to take Misty to the eye specialist," he told them.

They all filed out after saying their goodbyes and wishing her luck. Misty couldn't be happier. The fur was so nice under her feet, and the quilt was soft. She moved to put on her riding boots and knew Brody was watching her.

"You like it," Brody sighed. "Figures," he grumbled. "Cassie and Ali liked their rooms too."

Then he took her hand and led her out to his bike. He strapped her helmet on her head, then climbed on. She reached out, and grabbed his shoulders, then climbed on behind him. Once she had her arm wrapped around him, he started the bike and turned to kiss her head.

"You in any pain back there," he asked in concern.

"I'm just fine," she told him.

Her arm hurt a bit where it rested against his back, but she wasn't telling him that. They had an argument earlier because he wanted to take the truck. She wanted no part of it. As long as she could hold on to him with one arm, and not fall off, she would ride. He had finally agreed, happy she liked riding on the back of his bike so much.

She heard Shadow start his bike, and she smiled as she looked over at him. The only consolation had been that Shadow ride with them. That way he could follow and let Brody know if she was having trouble. Her big bad Biker, was super protective. She smiled as they pulled out.

Chapter Thirty Two
Trike

Trike pulled into the parking lot of the hospital and found a spot near the door. He helped Misty off the Harley and then took her hand to lead her inside. The specialist was on the third floor, so they headed for the elevators, with Shadow trailing behind them. He kissed Misty's head, as the elevator dinged to let them know it had arrived. The three of them stepped inside.

"You're an awfully strong girl to go through all this," Shadow said from the corner. "I admire you," he told Misty.

"Thanks Shadow," she whispered. "I appreciate you saying that."

Then the door opened, and they headed down the hall. Trike found the right room and pushed inside. Misty followed him in, but Shadow signalled he'd wait in the hall. Trike nodded his thanks and moved into the office. The room looked just like a normal eye doctors would be, except there was a huge desk in the corner.

"Misty honey," the doctor said as he headed their way. Then Trike heard him gasp. "My dear, what happened to you?"

"I had an accident, nothing too serious," she told him. "I'll be fine in a couple days," she said.

Trike frowned, but said nothing otherwise.

"Well I hope so," the doctor said with concern. "Now, lets sit at the desk and you can tell me what's happened, and how your sight has changed.

Trike sat beside Misty, and listened as she explained how she had fallen a couple days ago, and hit her head. Then she explained how she had awakened after, and how things looked. She also told him she hadn't been suffering any dizziness, or bad headaches since it had happened.

The doctor seemed pleased, and explained that sometimes it's as simple as just hitting it again, to get the sight to come back. He was adamant she would most likely regain her sight completely, but it would be gradually.

Next, he took her over to the machines, and tested her sight in lots of different ways. He shined lights in her eyes, he put drops in them, and he had her try to make out images on some charts. Then he had her sit behind a machine with different lenses as he tried hundreds on her. After about a half hour, he was done.

They returned to the desk, and he told her he was extremely pleased. Her sight had improved almost sixty-five percent. That number was high for such a short amount of time. Also, with that number, he felt her sight might come back quicker than he thought.

Trike watched as his girl struggled with tears. He knew she hadn't expected the doctor to say that. He took her hand and squeezed it, giving her his strength and encouragement. Trike was happy for her, and he wanted her to know it.

Next, the doctor explained he wanted to take Misty down the hall so he could take some X-rays. Misty agreed, and they stood up. Since Trike wasn't allowed in the room with her, he and Shadow waited down the hall in a sitting room. They could get a coffee while they waited for her.

The doctor explained it would most likely take about twenty minutes, and then he'd bring her back. Trike took Misty's cell phone to hold onto and kissed her goodbye. He told the doctor where he would wait, and the doctor promised to bring her right to him, as soon as they were done.

He watched her walk away, then motioned to Shadow to follow him. They sat in the small waiting room and drank coffee as they waited. Trike didn't know the prospect we'll, so he was happy to have time alone with him. Shadow talked about his time in the military, explaining he had been a Navy Seal, and it impressed Trike. They got along well, and Trike liked the brother.

Forty-five minutes later, there was still no Misty. Both Trike and Shadow looked at each other, knowing something was wrong. Trike roared as he ran down the hall, searching for his girl, but he had a gut feeling, he wouldn't find her.

Chapter Thirty Three
Misty

Misty hated getting X-rays done. She sat in the chair
and held still as it took the pictures. The doctor had
put special clamps on her lids to keep them open. It
wasn't painful, just really uncomfortable. The
specialist took several pictures from all different
angles. When he was satisfied, he removed the clamps
and asked her to blink several times before he turned
on all the lights.

Her eyes ran as she blinked, then she closed them
tightly as the lights came on. It stung, even with them
closed. She thanked the doctor as he helped her out of
the chair. He told her they were all done, and he'd
take her back to Brody.

The doctor pulled open the door, then stumbled back, as they pushed him into the room. Misty cried out as they knocked her and she fell to the floor. Luckily it was her left side that hit. She looked up as three people entered. She recognized Carly right away, but didn't know the two men with her.

One man hit the doctor over the head with something, and she watched in shock as he slumped to the floor. Then, the other man grabbed her arm, and hauled her to her feet. She opened her mouth to scream, but he clamped his hand over it.

"Oh no you don't," he said into her ear. She knew immediately, this was the man that had threatened her before. She tried to pull away, but he only tightened his grip on her. "I'm gonna move my hand, and you will not make a sound. If you do, I'll shoot you," he growled.

She nodded she understood, and he took his hand away. Tears streamed down her face as a gun was thrust into her side. Then she was pushed towards the door again. Carly and the other man flanked her, as they headed down the hall, in the opposite direction as the sitting room Trike and Shadow were in.

Someone opened a door, and then they were hurrying down three flights of stairs. She stumbled a couple times, and it was hard to see, as her eyes were a bit sore from the tests, and the tears. The man kept a tight hold on her though, so she never fell.

When they reached the door, he growled at her to keep her head down, before pushing it open. They crossed the front reception area, with no problems, and headed out the automatic doors. She sobbed outright then, as they headed through the parking lot, and away from Brody. She did not understand how long Brody would wait in the sitting room before he'd go looking for her.

They reached a black van, and Carly opened the back doors. The man roughly pushed her forward, then followed her in. She moved as far away from him as she could and sat down. He sat across from her and raised his knees. He placed the gun on them, so it pointed directly at her.

"Why," she whispered to him, as the van started up, then moved.

He tilted his head as he studied her. "Those fucking bikers kicked me and my buddy out of the club when I was prospecting. Somebody got away, and they blamed us. It was pure luck when I met Carly. We were fucking for six months, and no one knew. Then surprise, surprise, when I saw Trike pick you up one day. Made my fucking day. It was the asshole who got patched in when we didn't. And Carly was pissed at Noah for cutting her off, so here we are," he sneered.

"We get to hurt two people at once, plus the club, and it only takes one small blind bitch to get it done," he said.

Misty turned away from him and leaned back in the corner. She could only pray that it didn't take Trike long to find her. She needed him now because she had no idea what they had planned for her.

Chapter Thirty Four
Trike

Trike tore down the hall, like the hounds of hell were on his heels. He found the X-ray room and shoved the door open. There on the floor, lay the specialist that Misty was supposed to be with. He had blood on his temple, and he was unconscious. Shadow pushed past him and checked for a pulse after a minute he nodded.

Trike move again then and hurried back out the door. Shadow cursed and followed him. They ran in the opposite direction as they were sitting. The knew she didn't pass so that made the decision easy. They found the stairwell and barrelled down it, coming out through the reception area. There was no sign of Misty. Trike ran out the front doors and into the parking lot, but it was no use, his girl was gone.

"Fuck," he roared as he slammed his first down on top of the nearest car. He heard Shadow talking on the phone behind him, but he ignored him. What the hell was he going to do now. He had promised Noah he'd look after her, and now she was missing. He roared again as he paced in front of the cars.

"Trike, we need to move fast. Let's question the staff on that floor, and see if they have any cameras stationed that we can pull the feed from," he ordered. Trike nodded, at least now he had somewhere to start.

They went back upstairs and reported the doctors injuries to the nurses. A stretcher was brought in, and they took the doctor out. They then showed them where the security cameras were placed in the halls and stairs. They would definitely be on tape, they just had to find them.

Minutes later Steele and Dragon arrived, so the four of them headed to the security office. They watched the tapes and saw Misty being dragged down the stairs. It was clear Carly was with her, but what infuriated the bikers, was the two prospects they had kicked out months before. This was payback, and none of them were happy about it.

They got more security tapes and discovered the black van that the men had taken Misty away in. Luckily, there was a clear view of the licence plate. Dragon pulled out his phone and called the two detectives, telling them they needed them at the hospital.

Twenty minutes later, the detectives arrived, and were filled in on what was going on. They watched the video, and wrote down the license plate, then headed off to see what they could dig up.

"Head back to the compound, we'll have church and get things moving," Steele ordered. Trike wasn't happy, but he knew without knowing where they had taken Misty, it would be a wild goose chase. She could be absolutely anywhere.

The brothers mounted up, and rode back to the compound, heading straight in to church. Preacher was there, along with the rest of the club, and they looked up as Trike prowled in.

"We'll get her back brother," Preacher promised. Then he threw two files on the table. "This is what I have on the two prospects," he said. He was about to say more, but a knock came on the door. He rose and opened it, and Trike was surprised to see Mario stride in.

"Now I know church is for bikers only, but Mario has more connections than we do. We need all the help we can get," he said. The brothers nodded, so Mario took a seat. Trike looked at him and tipped his head in thanks.

"I'll do everything I can," he promised. "My men are already tapping into the traffic cams, to see if they can locate the van. I have them all on standby, and they're and ready to move," he told them.

"Appreciated," Trike said.

Then the brothers put their heads together and began to plan. His girl was coming home tonight, and then they would cut the prospects to pieces. When he was done, there'd be nothing left of them.

Chapter Thirty Five
Misty

Misty was terrified. When the van doors shut, it was dark in the back, and she couldn't see a thing. Thank god, the man with her stayed on his side, and left her alone. She prayed silently for Brody. She had just found him, and she didn't want to lose him.

They drove on, and Misty did not understand where they were taking her. She listened carefully, trying to pick up some clues. In a small town, it was quiet, so there wasn't much to pick up on. She knew they were headed out of town because she didn't hear many cars anymore.

Then, she heard thousands of tiny pings on the bottom of the ground. That meant they were on the back roads outside town. The pings were probably the loose gravel pieces hitting the bottom of the van. She figured they were either heading for the woods, or to some abandoned cabin. She didn't know which terrified her more.

Suddenly, the van rocked hard, and she slammed her bad arm against the side. The pain caused her to whimper, and she was quick to move, and lean a different way. It threw her back and forth as the van drove over hundreds of bumps. Misty was sure they had left the road now.

Eventually, the van seemed to slow down, and finally it came to a stop. Misty was happy the van had finally stopped, but she really didn't want to get out. The way Carly was acting, it was safer to stay where she was.

She had no choice though, when the back doors were opened, and Carly stood there, yelling at her to get out. She looked over to see the man with the gun, moving towards her. Misty cowered in the corner, curling her body around her bad arm. The man grabbed her hair and dragged her across the van floor to the door.

Then he let go and issued an ultimatum. "You can climb out yourself darling, or I can give you a shove, your choice," he sneered.

Misty wasn't taking any chances. She spun around and let her legs hang out the back. Then, she gave a little jump, and landed on the ground. The man followed her out and slammed the doors behind them.

Misty took a minute to look around. They were on an old dirt road that was badly grown over and full of pot holes. She could see a sign up ahead, but her eyes weren't good enough to read it. After the sign was a clearing, but she recognized nothing.

Nobody said a word, but Carly turned and walked down the old road. It got worse ahead, which she figured was why they stopped driving. The man with the gun grabbed her good arm and dragged her in the direction Carly had taken. After about fifteen minutes they stopped.

"This is the old mine," Carly said as she turned towards her. "We will lead you in, then leave you there. With all the twists and turns, and without your sight, you'll never find your way out," she laughed.

"What about my brother," Misty asked in shock.

Carly laughed. "I'm done with him. I've got a new man," she said, as she walked over to the man with the gun and kissed him. "This here's Keith, and his buddies name is Adam. Did you know at one time they were prospects for the club? Only, they were kicked out, so when we hooked up, we realized we could kill two birds with one stone. Trike will be devastated when he finds you're dead body, and in turn the club with be devastated. Also, Noah will realize that he should have married me long ago, and he'll regret that too. It's a loose, loose for everybody," she laughed.

Adam, the other man who had been with them the whole time, shuffled on his feet. "I don't know about this," he said. "I don't need the club coming after me," he said.

Misty felt a bit of hope. Maybe Adam would stop them from doing this, she thought. But she wasn't that lucky, Carly took the gun off Keith, and shot Adam in the side. The man fell to his knees, clutching his side.

Chapter Thirty Six
Trike

Trike was beyond furious. It had been two hours since they had taken Misty, and they hadn't found her yet. All the brothers were out looking, along with Mario's men and the detectives. Mario's men had hacked the traffic cams, and they had tracked the van through town, then lost them.

That put them heading south out of town, but that wasn't much to go on. The van was never spotted again after that. They traveled all the back roads, and talked to everyone they saw along the way, and still came up dry.

It worried Trike. His girl still didn't have her sight back fully, it was getting dark, and she still had some serious injuries. Trike's phone was ringing off the wall with updates, but none of the news was good. He wanted someone to call and tell him they found her.

His phone rang again, and in frustration, he answered with, "what." There was silence for a minute, and then he barely made out Noah's voice.

"Something wrong," Misty's brother asked.

"Fuck me," he swore. "I called you over an hour ago, but you didn't answer. Did you get my message," he asked.

"I've been on a good damned plane since this morning. I land in forty-five minutes. This is the first time I've got reception. I called my sister to let her know I was coming, but she never answered."

"Fuck me," Trike roared again. "You got your sniper rifle with you," he asked.

"Always," Noah answered.

"Carly, and a couple prospects we kicked out a while ago, kidnapped your sister. I have half the god damned town out looking for her, and I could use you," he growled.

"Fuck me," Noah roared.

"I already said that," Trike smart mouthed back.

"Right," Noah huffed. "Thank god my paperwork got pushed through. I should hit town in an hour. I'll call again when I'm there, and you better have a location for me to head to," he said furiously. "I'll be locked and loaded."

"Just the way I need you," Trike said as he hung up. At least that was one good call he'd got.

A half hour later he got another promising call. Dagger called to let him know they had spotted the van way out of town, close to the old mine. Trike immediately pushed the throttle and headed that way. All the brothers, and Mario's men converged at a cross road about fifteen minutes from the mine.

As soon as he stopped, Noah called again, so Trike told him where they were. The men knew there was nothing but the mine out there so that was where they figured Misty would have been taken. They decided to split up and come at it from different directions.

Just as they were leaving, a bike came roaring down the road. It was extremely loud, and extremely fast, and it caught everyone's attention. As it got closer, Trike sighed in relief. On it, was a man dressed in camo, and strapped to his back was a long bag that could only hold a sniper rifle.

Trike immediately signalled, and Noah turned and headed straight for him. When he stopped the bike and dismounted, Trike moved to him and shook his hand, introducing himself. Trike was surprised to see how large Noah was, considering how tiny Misty was.

Trike was about to introduce him to everyone when a shot rang out. It was a ways away, but they all recognized it for what it was. As a group the bikers ran for their bikes, and Mario's men jumped in their cars. Then a huge procession headed in the direction of the gunshot.

Trike hoped that gunshot hadn't been aimed at Misty, because with the amount of fire power all the men with him were carrying, it was gonna be a blood bath.

Chapter Thirty Seven
Misty

Misty watched in horror as Carly shot Adam in the side. He roared, as he clutched at the wound and fell to the ground. Misty took a step back, just trying to get away from Carly, but Carly turned towards her.

"Don't you dare move, or I'll shoot you too," she threatened. Misty stopped, not wanting to provoke her. "Good girl," Carly snarled. "Keith get the dynamite and set it up," she ordered.

"Carly, what are you doing," she whispered. But Carly didn't say a word, she motioned for Keith to get started.

Keith took a backpack off his shoulder and headed to the entrance of the mine. He set it down and pulled out three sticks of dynamite that had been wrapped together. Misty could only watch in horror as he shoved the sticks into the loose rocks at the side of the opening.

Misty cried out, as Carly grabbed her arm, and pulled her towards the mine. She struggled, then kicked out at Carly's knee. Carly let go of her arm and leaned down to grab her knee. Misty took advantage and kicked her again, this time catching her in the side.

Carly turned as she screamed and pointed the gun at her. She didn't even have time to move as Carly fired. A burning pain shot through her leg, and she fell. She sobbed, as she clutched at the spot the bullet had entered.

During the commotion, no one was watching Adam, and Misty stared at the man, as he climbed in the van and started it up. He pounded his chest, then pointed right at her. The roar of the vehicle got both Carly and Keith's attention. Carly fired at it, as Keith yelled threats, but it was no use, the van was quickly pulling away.

Carly cursed, then stomped over and pulled Misty to her feet once more. Misty screamed as the pressure on her leg caused to fall again. This time Keith came over. He picked up Misty and carried her into the mine.

"That fucker just fucked us over," he bellowed as he walked. "No way all those gun shots weren't heard, and how the hell do we get out of here now," he angrily asked.

"We'll figure it out, but we gotta move fast now," Carly said.

They finally dropped Misty in the dirt, quite a way into the mine. Then both Carly and Keith turned and hurried back to the entrance. Misty couldn't see well as it was dark in the mine and her eyesight still wasn't great. She knew her leg was bad though, so she unwrapped the sling from her arm, and tied it around her thigh, hoping that would help the bleeding. Her arm hurt too, but she couldn't do anything about that.

She tried to stand several times, using the wall to try to pull herself up, but it was no use. Even though she got up, her leg wouldn't hold her weight, and she'd slide back down the rough walls. She screamed and screamed, begging someone to help her.

Suddenly, a small flare glowed at the end of the tunnel, and then a huge explosion went off. Misty screamed again, and covered her head, as bits of dirt rained down on her. She coughed several times as the dust from the explosion filled her mouth. She pulled at her t-shirt and covered her face as best she could.

When the dust cleared, she pulled the shirt away. The entire mine was pitch black, and she couldn't see a thing. Carly and Keith had effectively sealed the entrance, with her inside. She didn't know what to do as she had no way to let Trike know where she was. Misty could only hope that someone had heard the huge blast, and they'd come to check it out.

She thought of Adam again and prayed he'd help her. She hoped that's what he was trying to tell her before he drove away. Misty had to believe he'd tell someone where she was, if not, she knew she'd die here.

Chapter Thirty Eight
Trike

Trike roared down the dirt lane on his motorcycle, with a ton of bikes and cars following. The road was atrocious. It was terribly overgrown and narrow, which meant they almost had to go single file. Trike prayed that Misty was at the end, and that she was okay, because there would be hell to pay if she wasn't. But, the gunshot he heard had him terrified.

Suddenly, more gunshots filled the air, and Trike gripped the steering wheel tighter. All he could do was pray that Misty was okay, but by how many shots he heard, he knew it wasn't likely.

He pushed the bike as fast as he could, with Noah right at his back. He felt for Misty's brother. The poor man had suffered by not being able to help her before. He hoped he could hold his shit together for a while longer.

Trike saw dust rising in the distance, then he was forced to slow, as a van came barreling towards them with the horn blaring. Trike growled, as he knew right away the van was the same one that had been used in the kidnapping.

He screeched to a stop, as did everyone else, when the van got close. It barely braked before someone was screaming from the inside. Trike drew his gun, and used his bike as cover, when the van door was thrown open. He was furious when he saw the old prospect, Adam, step out.

He almost fired he was so angry, but forced himself to reign it in. Adam was bellowing his name, and he noticed the man's side was covered in blood. He yelled at the bikers behind him to hold their fire, knowing all of them would have their guns drawn as well.

Trike stepped in front of his bike. "I'm here," he called. "And you have seconds before I finish the job someone obviously started," he threatened.

"Misty's at the mine," he blurted. "Carly shot her in the thigh and she's dragging her inside. Keith plans to blow the entrance and seal her in. You have minutes until that happens," he told them in almost one breath.

"Why are you helping us now," Trike roared.

"I didn't mean for Cassie to get hurt. I felt terrible about it, and I'm trying to fix it. I messed up with her, but I'll do what I can for Misty," he promised. "I know it won't save me from the club, but at least I'll be able to live with myself," he signed.

Trike only nodded. "Move the van out of the god damned way. Then follow us back to the mine. Doc can help you while we work on freeing Misty."

Adam said nothing, just jumped back in the van, and drove it right into the trees. All the brothers mounted again, and were about to take off, when a huge explosion shook the ground. Smoke rose into the air from further down the lane. Trike felt his heart literally stop as he stared at the sight in horror.

"Move that god damned bike," Noah roared at him, "or I'll drive right over it."

Trike shook his head to clear his thoughts, then he let his anger take over. He twisted the throttle, and the tires spun, then he was flying down the lane. The roar of the bikes behind him, made the ground shake.

He leaned to the side as he took each corner recklessly, praying the bike stayed upright. All it would take was one rock or loose patch of dirt, for him to lose control. A dirt bike would have been better suited for this road.

Trike held his breath as he took the final turn and came up on the mine. He stopped his bike in anguish as he saw the front of the mine had been caved in by the explosion. If Misty was inside, she may be dead. She already had some serious wounds, but add to that a gunshot, and being buried alive, and he didn't know how she could survive. All he could do was pray now.

He was ripped from his thoughts when a bullet hit the tree right beside his head. He growled, as he pulled his own gun and returned fire. Misty's life was at stake, and he didn't have time for this.

Chapter Thirty Nine
Trike

Trike had no idea where the shooter was firing from. It seemed to be only one person. He knew it was near the mine, but he couldn't pinpoint the location. His brothers all hunkered down and returned fire. He saw some of them break off, and head in different directions, trying to surround the shooter. He assumed the shooter was Keith, but he didn't know if Carly was with him or not.

Suddenly, he heard a movement above him. He looked up, stunned to see Noah climbing the tree, with his sniper rifle strapped to his back. The brother was already halfway up, and the fucker was fast.

"Hey," Steele yelled up at him. When he had Noah's attention, he yelled, "no kill shots. Shoot to disable only, we have our own way of extracting vengeance."

Noah nodded once, then his focus returned to the tree, as he continued to climb. Trike hoped the man ended up joining the club, his skills would be quite the asset.

Time was of the essence, with Misty trapped inside. He tried to figure out where the shots were coming from when he thought he saw movement from the top corner. He concentrated all his shots there and saw his brothers were doing the same thing.

Suddenly, one loud shot rang through the air, and a scream followed it. Trike stood up in awe as he watched a man fall down the side of the hill. When he turned Shadow was there, but Trike wasn't surprised, the prospect was always appearing out of thin air.

"Damn good shot," he said.

Then Steele was there, yelling up into the tree, Noah was coming down from. "I thought I said to disable the fucker only."

Noah shrugged, after he jumped the last ten feet to the ground. "I did, it's not my fault the guy was standing on a hill."

Steele shook his head, as he stormed away toward the fallen man, ordering Shadow to follow.

"I need a couple men to hunt down Carly," Noah said. "I'm not rational right now, and my focus needs to be on Misty," he ordered.

Mario stalked up then. "If you can spare Navaho, I'll send some of my boys with him. He's the best bet we have, but I'm staying here. I figure we got a couple hours tops, to dig your girl out," he said.

"Done," Trike said. He turned to Navaho, but he had already overheard, and was headed away with Mario's men. Carly wasn't gonna get far if Navaho was tracking her.

Trike turned then, and headed for the mine, with Noah beside him, and Mario and his brothers behind him. They moved down the hill at a fast clip and surveyed the area.

"Dagger," Trike called. As soon as the brother got close, he asked. "You know dynamite. Can we blow the side," he asked.

"Nope. That mines way to unstable after the first blast. Another one will bring the roof down for sure," he explained.

Trike watched as Noah walked away and headed straight to the mine. Then he bent and physically moved the rocks away from the entrance with his hands. Within minutes, the entire club was beside him, along with Mario and his crew. Trike pushed forward, and roared, as he lifted one of the bigger rocks.

Five minutes later the detectives arrived, and without a word, they also joined in. They stopped for only a minute, when Shadow and Steele showed up with a dirty, but very much alive Keith.

Steele just glared at them. "This one got away, and you couldn't find him," he said furiously. The detectives immediately raised their hands in surrender, agreeing with the brother. Steele nodded, then dragged Keith to the front of the van Adam had driven back, and handcuffed him to the bumper. Trike didn't even ask where he got the cuffs.

Trike had forgotten about Adam, but when he turned, he found him working beside doc, and hauling rocks with a bloody side.

Then everyone stopped and turned when they heard screaming. Navaho appeared, walking out of the trees with Carly thrown over his shoulder, and Mario's men following. She was kicking and cursing until Navaho threw her in the dirt.

"What do you want done with this piece of trash," he asked.

Chapter Forty
Trike

Trike watched as Carly's face paled, as she looked around at all the bikers and Mario's men. They now had a system going, where they worked in an assembly line fashion, and concentrated on one area. There was five men at the front, lifting the rocks away, and then passing them back. This meant they were moving a lot faster.

As soon as the opening was big enough, Trike was going in. There was no way he would stay out here any longer while she was in there all alone. He was desperate to see if she was okay. It was the not knowing that was killing him.

It looked like Carly finally noticed Noah because she frantically screamed his name. He simply ignored her and kept digging. The waterworks started then as huge sobs racked her body. She was begging him now and pleading with him to help her. Finally, she screamed about how much she loved him, and everything she did was for him.

That got his attention. He threw the rock down and stomped over to her. Immediately, Shadow was there to take his place. Trike watched out of the corner of his eye as he kept working.

"You did this for me," he growled. "You ditched by blind sister at the lake at night, you moved the furniture causing her to fall into a glass table, you kidnapped her, shot her, and blew up a mine to trap her inside. How the fuck is this supposed to help me," he bellowed.

She smiled sweetly up at him, with tears still streaming down her face. "But with her out of the way, we can live the life we wanted. We can get married, we can buy the house with the white picket fence, and we can have two kids," she said happily. "You came home and I'm ready to start my life with you."

"Are you fucking serious," he roared. "My sister means the world to me. It fucking gutted me, to go back to Afghanistan and leave her, when she needed me the most. I loved you, and I put my trust in you, to keep my baby sister safe. I left the only surviving family I had, in your care. She fucking needed me, and I walked away, because they ordered me to, and because I knew you'd look after her," he said while barely holding on.

"If you've killed her, I swear to god, I'll kill you too. But, being in the marines for so long I've learned a few things, and I can promise you that your death will be slow, and filled with a shit ton of pain," he promised.

She visibly paled as she looked up at him. "But I love you," she cried.

"Well that sucks for you," he said, as he moved back to the mine, and got back to work. It looked like they were close to breaking through soon.

The detectives stepped forward then. "Carly you're under arrest, for theft of the van, for the kidnapping of Misty, for the illegal use of a firearm, for the illegal use of an explosive, for the attempted murder of Adam, and for the attempted murder, and possibly murder of

Misty," he stated. "And for whatever else we can come up with," he added.

"Not for twenty-four hours," Preacher bellowed from the top of the mine. "You can have her after that," he ordered.

"How the hell do we explain that," one detective roared back.

"She hit you and got away," he roared back, eyeing the six foot two detective, who was built like a linebacker.

The surrounding men snorted as Preacher and the detectives eyed each other. "Fine," one of them said, as he raised his hands in surrendered. "But there better be something left of her to bring before a judge," he said.

Preacher said not a word as he turned and walked away.

Chapter Forty One
Misty

Misty was cold. The dirt she was sitting in was cold, the rock walls were cold, and the darkness was cold. Her arm hurt, and her leg throbbed. She thought that when you got shot; you went numb after a while, but her leg just kept on hurting.

She thought about Brody and hoped he found love again after she was gone. He was still young, and he was such a great guy, he shouldn't have trouble in that department. She hoped that he never forgot about her.

Then she thought about Noah. Her brother was an amazing man. She hoped Carly hadn't made him fearful of loving again. Add to that, losing her and their parents two years ago, and she had no idea how he'd deal with it all. She hoped that when he came home, he found Brody and the club. The club would take care of him and help him heal. He'd need a new family.

Misty thought about her life. She had nothing to complain about. She had had a wonderful childhood with her parents and her brother. And before the accident, she had made a decent living with her photography business. And last, she had found love. She loved Brody, and knew that if she had have gotten out of this, she would have wanted to stay with him forever.

She thought about the accident she had been in with her parents and wondered why she was spared. Sure, she had met Brody, and she had treasured her time with him, but to die like this. The accident had taken out her parents on impact, and she had only lost her sight. But to die inside a cold, dark mine, with a bullet lodged in her leg, was something out of a movie. Things like this didn't happen in real life, at least not that she had ever heard about.

She at least hoped Brody's club or the detectives, found Carly and Keith. And, she hoped that Adam had gotten away. He hadn't hurt her, and she hoped that he was trying to signal to her when he left. Maybe, he'd find Brody and tell him where her body was.

She was getting tired, and she figured that meant that she was running out of air. She didn't panic, because it wasn't painful, but she thought that she'd be coughing a lot, and having trouble breathing. This was so much easier though.

Her leg was hurting less, and her eyes were getting heavy. She fought it, but it was getting hard. She hoped that when she died, her parents would be there waiting for her. Misty missed them and knew that one day she'd see Brody and Noah again.

Misty tipped her head back against the cold stone and closed her eyes. She knew that once she gave in, she'd be done for, but the pull was just too strong. She smiled as she pictured what she could of Brody in her mind. Misty wished she had gotten her sight back, and could have seen him completely just once. She wanted a complete picture of him to remember him by.

She could feel herself tipping over, but she couldn't help it, as she fell to the dirt floor. It didn't hurt, so she wasn't worried. She could feel the tears slide down her cheek, but she didn't have the energy to brush them away.

Then, she heard Brody call her name. It felt so real that she figured she must be dead now. She opened her eyes and knew for sure now that she was dead. There was darkness all around him, but he was high up near the roof of the tunnel and light surrounded him. That was how she knew, that, and the fact that she could see him completely. She could make out every detail of his face. She closed her eyes again, happy that she got to see him that way.

"Open your fucking eyes beautiful, because I didn't dig through this pile of rock to watch you die," Brody yelled.

She blinked, and opened her eyes again, but he was still there, and this time he was climbing down towards her.

Chapter Forty Two
Misty

Misty was having trouble keeping her eyes open as she watched Brody climb down the rubble inside the cave. She wanted to close her eyes, but she didn't want to lose sight of him. He was quick even though she could tell he was being careful.

She couldn't get her head around the fact that he could be real, and that she could actually see him. She closed her eyes for a second, but then she felt his hands on either side of her face.

"Come on beautiful, open your eyes. I need to see them, so I know you're with me," he pleaded.

"I'm always with you," she whispered. She watched as a huge smile graced his face. "You have a stunning smile," she told him. Then she noticed a small scar on one of his eyebrows. "You have a scar," she told him.

She watched as one of his hands reached up and touched his eyebrow. "You can see my scar," he asked in awe.

"I can see all of you", she said, smiling up at him. Then the tiredness took over again, and she closed her eyes.

"Oh no you fucking don't," he growled, as he picked her up. She cried out in pain, but still snuggled into his warmth.

"Cold," she whispered.

"I know honey, but I'll have you warm in just a minute." Then he was moving towards the pile of rubble again. He took a minute to scale it, and then they were at the top.

"I need to hand you off to someone, so they can pull you through," he explained. "We both won't fit together, the holes tiny," he explained. She cried quietly.

"I don't want to leave your arms," she pleaded.

"Come on monkey," she heard yelled from the opening. "Let go of pretty boy, and let me help you."

Her head flew in the direction of the voice, and she sobbed. There, poking his head through the hole, was Noah.

"Noah," she cried, as she tried to reach for him. Her arm barely moved, and she got frustrated.

"It's okay," Brody said soothingly. "I'll pass you to him, you don't need to do a thing." Then she was transferred from Brody's arms to Noah's, as she moved out of the mine.

Noah made his way down the side of the rocks, with Brody holding his arm, just in case he slipped. She stared up at her brother the whole time. When they got to the bottom, she buried her face in his neck and sobbed.

"You're okay monkey, I've got you," he kept repeating.

"I love you Noah, I've missed you so much." she sobbed. He pulled her back, so he could look into her face.

"I love you too monkey, and I'm here to stay," he told her.

"Brody," she called as she turned to look for him, but he was right beside her. "This is my brother Noah," she told him happily.

"I know honey," he chuckled. "We've already met." Then he leaned down and kissed her cheek. "We need to let Doc look at you," he told her.

"I like your outfit," she told Noah. "Camo suits you."

Noah stared down at her in awe. "You can see," he asked. She nodded her head.

"It's been coming back slowly, but I can see just as good as before," she explained.

He laughed and hugged her. "I'm happy for you monkey," he told her.

Misty took a minute to look around and saw people surrounded them. There were lots of bikers, and lots of men in suits. She sat up a little, and her body cooperated this time, so she reached out and grabbed onto Brody's shirt. He smiled at her as she pulled him close.

"Thank you," she said to Brody and Noah. Then she turned to everyone gathered around. "Thank you so much for saving me," she said passionately, to the men.

Then she laughed, embarrassed, as a roar of cheers went up from everyone around her. She smiled as she squirmed to get closer to Brody while still holding onto Noah.

"Things will be okay," she said, as both men grinned her.

Chapter Forty Three
Trike

It surprised Trike when one of the first things Misty
did, when she was freed from the mine, was to thank
everyone. She had been barely breathing, and she still
had a bullet in her leg, but she had thought of the
people that had saved her. She didn't understand yet
that she was family, and this was what came with it.

Trike was thrilled she was alive. He had been so afraid
when he saw her slumped over, with her eyes closed.
He had loved the reaction she had when she saw Noah
too. You could easily see the love they had for each
other, and he loved that she had that.

Doc came to his side then, with his medical bag in his
hand. He checked her arm, and declared it needed

some stitches replaced, and a really good cleaning to get all the dirt out. Then he unwrapped the sling from her leg. He said that with the bullet still in there; the bleeding wasn't as bad as it could have been, but the bullet needed to come out.

Doc wanted her to go to the hospital, but both her and her brother hated hospitals, after the accident. Doc relented and said he had removed bullets before at the clubhouse, and although he disagreed with it, he could do it with no problems. That seemed to relieve Misty a lot.

Mario came over then and introduced himself to Misty. She thanked him and made him lean down so she could kiss his cheek. Trike just growled at him, until his girl slapped his shoulder, and told him to knock it off. Some bikers that overheard them snickered, but he glared at them all.

Mario then offered to cart Carly and Keith to the clubhouse for them. Trike cringed as Misty visibly paled.

"They're here," she asked him. Trike had no choice but to nod and point the couple out that had been handcuffed to the bumper of the van. He watched as she turned to Noah, with tears in her eyes.

"I'm so sorry," she told him. He kissed her forehead, then leaned down in her face.

"Don't you ever be sorry for my mistake. I left you with her, and she almost killed you. That's on me," he swore. Trike watched as she tried to smile, but it wouldn't come.

"Take me over to her," she ordered Trike.

"I don't think so," he roared in anger.

"I'll crawl," she threatened, as he watched her try to do just that. He looked at Noah, but the man just smirked at him. With no choice, he scooped her up and carried her over to Carly.

"I want her standing," she ordered Dagger who stood beside Carly. He unlocked the cuffs, then grabbed her arm, hauling her to her feet.

"You should have died," Carly sneered at her. "Your brother will see the error of his ways," she said, with pure confidence.

"Put me down, but please stand behind me and hold me up," she asked Trike. He did as she asked, putting her down, but standing behind her and taking all her weight.

"I think you will actually see the error of your ways," she told Carly. Then she hauled back her good arm and punched Carly in the face. Carly went down in a heap, and Dagger let her go, as she fell. The girl was clearly unconscious and was bleeding at the mouth.

"Where did you learn to hit like that," Mario asked. "And that was your left hand."

"My brothers a badass marine," she said smiling back at Noah. Noah just smirked at her, as all the surrounding men roared in laughter, as Trike picked her up again.

"Let's go home and get you fixed up," Trike told her.

"Home," she agreed. "I'd love that," she told him, then passed out in his arms.

Chapter Forty Four
Trike

Things moved quickly at the mine once Misty passed out. Doc said she was in no danger, she had just passed out from stress, exhaustion and her wounds. Mario offered to drive her and Trike back to the clubhouse himself, and Trike took him up on his offer. His men would make sure both Carly and Keith got to the clubhouse. The brothers would deal with them after Misty was looked after.

They gave Adam to the detectives. He wasn't under arrest, only, because he helped them locate Misty faster. Because of his actions, the club was letting him off. He wasn't welcome back though. He had messed up with Cassie, and that wouldn't be forgiven. The detectives were taking him to the hospital, to get patched up. It was also advised he leaves town and not return. Adam agreed and left on good terms.

The detectives were also taking in the van as evidence. They advised everyone to leave as they figured more police would arrive shortly. There was no way someone didn't call in that blast. The detectives understood that they wouldn't be getting Keith back, but they would be at the clubhouse at nine the next morning to collect Carly. They also advised to be careful what injuries were inflicted on her as they had to look like they occurred at the mine.

Once Trike was at the clubhouse, he took Misty to the room doc was using as his medical office. With all that had gone down in the past with the club women, and all the times Doc was needed, it made sense to give him a room he could use as a makeshift clinic. Doc was a valuable asset, and the brothers wanted him to know they appreciated him.

Trike laid Misty down on the exam table, and Doc got to work. He cleaned her leg, and within a half hour, had the bullet out, and the hole stitched shut. He then moved to her arm. Doc cleaned it good and stitched up a lot of the reopened wounds. Then he wrapped the whole thing in gauze and gave her a new sling.

Doc had given her a heavy sedative, before he started, so Misty would sleep the rest of the day away.

Trike carried her to his room and got her settled in his bed. He curled up with her for a bit, just holding her, and watching her as she slept. Then he called a prospect and had him sit outside his door while he went to check on a few thinks.

The first place he headed was the common room, and Noah was there like he'd hoped. He pulled out a bar stool and sat beside him.

"You settled in," he asked him. The brothers decided Noah should stay at the clubhouse, and they were hoping he'd consider joining up. Noah was a good man, and he'd be an asset to the club.

"Yep, I got what I brought with me, and I'm set up in Steele's old room. I'll go through all the stuff you brought back from the apartment in a day or so," he replied. "Appreciate you putting me and Misty up."

"Misty belongs with me," he told the brother, "so you do as well." Noah just nodded. "Besides, as soon as she's up I'm moving her to the cabin I built, down the back of the property. You're welcome to move in with us," he told him.

"Nope, Misty needs to live her own life. Besides, I like the clubhouse, and I like what I see. I wouldn't mind prospecting," he said.

Trike nodded, pleased. He was about to say more when Steele entered the room.

"Misty good," he bellowed across the room.

"She'll be asleep for a while," Trike yelled back.

"You ready to play," he asked.

"Fuck yes," Trike said, as he pushed away from the bar. Then he turned to Noah.

"You coming," he asked with a smile.

"Wouldn't miss it," Noah replied.

Then Trike headed outside, with Noah right behind him. Finally, it was time to end the man that had kidnapped his woman.

Chapter Forty Five
Trike

Trike pushed open the door of the shed and stopped. Dragon, Navaho, Dagger and Preacher greeted him. Steele and Noah stepped in behind him.

"Nice," Noah whistled, as he looked at Keith. As with everyone that had the unfortunate luck of being brought to the shed, Keith was bound in chains, and hanging from the ceiling. He had a gag in his mouth, but he was wide awake and glaring at them all.

The glare surprised Trike. The man had been a prospect of the club at one time, so he wasn't ignorant about what went on in here. Keith should be quaking in his boots right now, but maybe the man was even more stupid than they thought. No worries though, he wouldn't be glaring much longer.

Dagger walked towards Keith with his knife and sliced up his cheek, to remove the gag. Unfortunately, the slice went a little too deep, and Dagger chuckled.

"Whoops," he laughed. "My bad." Trike just shook his head at his brothers slip. And so it begins, he thought to himself.

Steele walked over to Noah and clapped him on the back. "I hear you're thinking of prospecting for the club," he asked.

"Was thinking about it," Noah told him. "I need to find somewhere I belong," he told them.

Preacher stepped forward then. "You belong with us," he said. "Consider this your initiation."

"Yes sir," Noah agreed.

"Just so you know, I'm not telling you shit," Keith said, butting in.

"That's good," Trike told him. "We don't need shit. We're here to kill you, and do it really slowly," he said, as he growled at the man. Keith paled, but kept his glare.

Dragon moved to Noah's side next. "You ever used a blowtorch before," he asked.

"Yeah," Noah answered. "But I don't think I use it for what you use it," he smirked.

"Well maybe you're just using it wrong," Steele countered.

"Oh, I know I'm using it right," Noah said back,

"Fuck me," Dagger said. "I don't think we're talking about a blowtorch anymore. Can we focus on killing this fucker," he growled.

"I think we should let them talk," Keith butted in with once again.

"Shut up," all the brothers said at once.

"You got a favourite tool," Steele asked Noah.

"My sniper rifle," Noah answered.

"Fine by me," Steele answered. Then he turned to Navaho and Dagger. "Get him down, and take him out to the back, where we have target practice. Secure him to a couple trees and make sure he's spread out. Noah, grab your sniper rifle, and meet Trike out front. He'll take you and set you up on the roof of the garage."

Preacher turned to Trike, "you good with this," he asked. Trike just nodded as he led Noah away.

Ten minutes later, they were set up on the roof, and Noah had Keith in his sights. The target was about eight hundred meters away, which Noah claimed was an easy shot. Most of his shots on the field, were between one thousand and fifteen hundred.

Trike watched as Noah lined up a shot, then squeezed the trigger. The bullet flew out of the gun and hit Keith in the arm. Trike pulled out his binoculars and saw Keith screaming, as his arm dangled, from where the bullet had half severed it. Noah lined up again, and another bullet flew from the rifle. This time it hit Keith's other arm.

Keith was slumped, and his eyes were glazed, but he was still awake, and frantically trying to free himself. Noah put another bullet in the chamber and fired once more. This time, the bullet tore through his calf, but unlike the others, it severed his foot completely. They could hear Keith screaming, even with the huge distance between them.

It took three more bullets, before Keith died, and even Trike had to look away near the end. It was an incredibly gruesome sight.

"Brother, swear to god, you got skills, but you terrify me," Trike told him honestly.

Noah just smirked at him, as he dismantled his weapon, and put it away. One down, Trike thought, and one to go.

Chapter Forty Six
Misty

Misty woke to someone calling her name. Slowly, she opened her eyes, then smiled as she saw Brody's face close to hers. She reached out with her good hand and pushed his hair out of his face.

"I'll never tire of looking at you," she said. "You take my breath away."

"I'm thinking you're stealing my lines," Brody laughed. "I'm so happy you can see baby," he told her. Then he kissed her, and it lasted a while. When he pulled away, she stared up at him happily.

"I used to take pictures," she blurted out.

"I know," Brody told her. "Your brother told me last night. I went through all the stuff we pulled out of the apartment and found all your camera equipment. I put it in a safe place until you're ready to use it again."

"Thank you," Misty said in surprise.

"You're welcome honey. How are you feeling," he asked.

"Sore," she admitted. "But relieved it's over. I thought I would die in there," she told him.

"I thought you were too," Brody admitted. "You just about scared me to death," he told her.

She smiled up at him. "So now we can be together," she asked.

"We were always together," he told her. "No matter what happened, or what you said, you were always mine," he said.

"Now what," she asked him. She watched as the smile left his face, and she got nervous.

"Now we need to talk," he told her.

"Where's my brother," she asked. Then took Brody's hand. She watched as the smile returned to his face.

"Your brothers in the common room," he told her. "We set him up in Steele's old room, and he wants to prospect for the club," he told her.

Misty threw herself into his arms. "He's staying, and he will be close by," she said.

"Yeah baby," Brody said as he held her. "Your brothers here for good, and so are you." She beamed up at him.

"Now," Brody said, "it's seven am. The detectives are coming at nine, to take Carly away. She's going to jail, and she's never coming out. That gives us two hours with her until we have to turn her over. We're allowed to hurt her, the only stipulation is that it has to look like it happened at the mine," Brody explained.

"What happened to Keith," she asked.

"I don't think you need to know that," Brody told her frowning.

"He kidnapped me, and buried me alive, I think I have a right to know," she retorted. She watched as he hung his head.

"We tied him to a tree, and Noah shot him with his sniper rifle. It took about eight shots to kill him," Brody admitted.

"Good," she said. "And we have two hours with Carly," she said. "I want my turn with her," she stated.

"Honey, you're hurting. We need to feed you and get pain meds into you," he said.

She ignored him and moved to the side of the bed. She grabbed his sweats that were on a chair beside the bed.

"Get me in these," she ordered. She watched Brody smirk, then with no argument, he moved to do as she asked. She stood and moved across the room. Brody was right beside her the whole time. Her leg was killing her, and she knew she was limping bad, but at least she could walk. She headed straight to the common room.

Everyone there stopped talking as she walked in. When she saw Noah, he hurried over to her, and wrapped her in his arms. They clung to each other for a minute before she let go.

"Navaho," she called, and the biker moved to her side. She motioned for him to bend down, and he snickered as he did as asked. She whispered a few things to him, and he nodded.

"Shadow, you're with me," he shouted, as he headed outside.

Misty turned to the two girls who sat in the corner.

"Care to help me bring on some hurt," she asked them.

"Hell yeah," they both said, as they jumped to their feet.

"Let's go get the bitch," she roared. Then she walked out, with a girl on each side, and the men chuckling behind her.

"I think I'm in love," she heard Brody say, before the door shut.

Chapter Forty Seven
Misty

Misty pushed the door of the shed open with her good arm and found Carly hanging from chains from the ceiling. She blinked at the sight, then giggled.

"What are you laughing at," Carly sneered. "I heard the detectives telling you not to hurt me, and they should be here shortly."

"Yep," Misty said. "But first, they said not to hurt you too bad, and to make it look like it happened at the mine. And two, they won't be here for about two hours."

"But you can't even see me, you bitch. You gonna get the big bad bikers to hurt me. When it gets out that they hurt a woman, they're finished," she screamed.

"Oh, the bikers aren't gonna hurt you, just me and my two best friends," she said.

"You can't touch me. Your brother loves me, and he won't let you near me," Carly sneered.

"Wrong sweetheart, but you'll figure that out eventually," Noah said from the doorway. Then he turned and walked away.

"Navaho," Misty called. In seconds, the big Indian appeared at the door. "Can you get her to where I want her," she asked.

Navaho nodded and stepped into the shed. A minute later, Carly was up and over his shoulder, and he was striding away. Misty turned and limped after her when she was scooped up by Brody. He didn't say a word, just followed Navaho.

When they arrived at the target area, Navaho dropped Carly to her feet. She turned to run, but smacked right into Shadow.

"Where are you going darling," he asked. Then he pulled her back to the trees and tied her up. She screamed and thrashed, but she was no match for the biker. Carly looked down and sobbed.

"Oh my god, is that a foot," she cried.

"Whoops, I guess we missed that," Shadow said, as he kicked it to the side. "Forget you saw that," he asked, like he was conspiring with her.

Her eyes bugged out, and tears ran down her face. "You're all crazy," she said.

"Nope, we're all bikers," Steele said coming up behind them. Misty looked back, and smiled as she saw most of the bikers standing behind them, with their arms crossed. They were all there for support. She kissed Brody's cheek, then asked him to put her down.

"You got everything," she asked Navaho. The biker pointed to the picnic table beside her.

Misty picked up one of the pellet guns, and handed it to Ali, then she handed the other one to Cassie. She watched as Navaho picked up a metal bucket and plunked it down over Carly's head. Then she turned to her new friends.

"I can't hold the gun myself, so I need your help. Please girls, fire away. Then hand your guns to Shadow, so he can reload them," she explained to them.

Ali and Cassie looked at each other a minute, then Ali shrugged and aimed the pellet gun at Carly. When the gun fired, a small pile of gravel shot out. It hit Carly in several places, causing her to cry out. Tiny spots of blood appeared on her arms and legs. It wouldn't cause a lot of damage, and it would hurt for a while, especially when the cuts were cleaned later.

Cassie laughed and picked up her gun too as Ali handed hers to Shadow. Misty smiled as Brody sat down at the picnic table and placed Misty on his lap.

"You're devious," he said without a hint of remorse. She tilted her face up and kissed him. Then they settled in to watch the show. Carly screamed and cursed them all from under her bucket as the girls continued to fire.

Twenty minutes later, most of the gravel was gone, and Carly was covered in tons of tiny wounds. It looked exactly like she had been too close to the blast.

"Okay ladies, round one is done. Round two is mine," she said. "Navaho can you tie her down to the picnic table," she asked. Then she grinned as she thought of what she would do next.

Chapter Forty Eight
Trike

Trike watched, as Navaho and Shadow removed the rope holding Carly to the tree, and dragged her to the picnic table. Carly still fought, but she had lost her attitude. She was struggling, but she wasn't cursing them all anymore.

Once the brothers had her flat on her back on the picnic table, they used the ropes that still dangled from her wrists, to tie her to the legs of the table. Trike watched, as the bikers moved back out of the way when she was secure. Misty stopped Shadow as he passed, and he handed her a small cup.

She then turned to Trike, and he smiled down at her. He kissed her forehead, then pushed her hair off her face.

"Can you remove my sling for just a minute," she asked him. Trike narrowed his eyes at her, but then gently undid the knot and pulled off the sling, shoving the end in his back pocket. Misty immediately walked up to Carly and stood beside her. Trike followed, and pressed his front to her back, wrapping one of his arms around her waist.

"You know, when I lost my sight in the accident, it terrified me. I never got to say goodbye to my parents, because it hurt too much, not being able to see them. Then Noah left, and I was all alone. You hated me and let me know it from the day he left. I needed help, and you refused to give it to me. I needed a friend, and you refused to be one," she whispered. Trike pulled her closer.

"Loosing my sight was like loosing a part of me. I couldn't do anything for myself, and I needed you. You do not understand what it's like to suddenly have your world go dark."

Noah stepped forward then and pulled Misty into his arms. "I'm sorry," he told her painfully.

"No," Misty growled, as she pushed away. "This is on her. You loved her, and you trusted her. You did nothing wrong." Then Trike watched, as she stood on tiptoes, and kissed her brothers cheek. Misty then turned back to Carly.

"When Noah and me were little, our parents took us to the beach. We played in the water, we built sand castles, and we had a picnic. It was a day I won't ever forget. But, what I remember most, is when Noah got sand in his eye. He rubbed at it, and it ended up scratching his eye. It was so bad, he had to wear a patch for a couple days, while it healed. He was fine, but for a while I was terrified for him," Misty said.

"Brody, can you help me, by holding open one of her eyes," she asked. Then she turned to Shadow and asked him to hold open the other one. Once he, and his brother were in position, Misty leaned down close to Carly's face.

"Being blind is life altering. It's scary, and it takes away all your independence. But, you never understood. I think you need to experience it for yourself, to see how bad I had it," she told Carly.

Trike watched, as Misty reached into the cup with her fingers, and pulled out a bit of the gravel. Then she sprinkled some in each eye. Carly screamed like a banshee and blinked several times.

"Steele," Misty called. When his brother had stepped up beside her, she asked if she could borrow his knife. Steele handed it over without a word. It was sharp, so it only took a second to cut each of the ropes holding Carly's wrists. As soon as she was free, she raised her hands and rubbed at her eyes.

"That's exactly what Noah did," Misty laughed. Carly was sitting up now as she kept rubbing. Even Trike knew she was making it worse. The more she rubbed, the more it would scratch her, and Misty had put in quite a bit.

"Help me," she yelled. "I can't open my eyes, it stings," she cried. They all watched, as Carly stood, and tried to find somebody to help. The girl hit another picnic table and cried out. After a minute, she gave up, and sat in the dirt, as she held her eyes and cried.

"I hope you remember how helpless you feel," Misty hissed at her. "Because it's something I'll never forget."

Chapter Forty Nine
Misty

Misty stared at Carly, and realized she wasn't upset at all, by what she had done. She had been a doormat for years, and she didn't want to be like that anymore. She had her whole life ahead of her, and her sight was back. She would never take that for granted again. Misty couldn't wait to get her camera out as everything looked new to her again.

Steele's cell rang then, and all the bikers turned to look at him. He answered it, grunted a couple times, and hung up.

"Detectives are here for Carly," he told them. "Let's get her to the gate."

Misty watched, as Navaho picked up Carly, and threw her over his shoulder. She snickered, as she saw that Carly didn't fight him at all, but continued to rub at her eyes, as she hung upside down.

Then Misty squealed as Brody picked her up too. But unlike Carly, he cradled her in his arms. "I can walk," she half protested.

She looked up to see Brody smirking at her. "Good one," he said. "Your limp is getting worse, and you haven't eaten or taken any pain meds. Your gonna stay right where you are pretty girl," he ordered.

She didn't protest at all, just snuggled in closer. He was right, she was hurting, but she had hoped nobody noticed. She should have known, she couldn't hide it from him. Every time she turned towards him, he was looking at her, and she loved it.

Finally, they reached the gate. Navaho dropped Carly on the ground as the detectives approached.

"What's the matter with your eyes," one detective asked, as he watched her rubbing them.

"There's dirt in them," Carly cried.

"Well stop fucking rubbing them," he told her. "You're gonna scratch them all to pieces."

The bikers snickered, and the detectives both looked at them, then they looked back down at Carly. Suddenly, both threw back their heads and laughed.

"Good one," one of them got out. When they had calmed down, they inspected her. "Was she in the blast," one asked.

"Yep," Brody replied. "Must have gotten too close."

The detectives didn't say a word. Of course, Carly did.

"They shot gravel at me with pellet guns," she roared, as she pointed to Ali and Cassie, who had followed them to the gate.

Both the detectives jaws dropped open, then they were laughing again.

"Pure genius," one stated. Then he turned serious. "Those two are a couple of the sweetest girls I know. It's not nice to falsely accuse them," he said. Then he ruined it by grinning.

"Just so you know, there's no trace of Keith. He must have gotten away," the other detective said. The brothers snickered, but Carly chose that minute to speak up again.

"His foot," she whispered. "I saw his foot."

The detectives both frowned down at her. "You saw his foot where," one asked.

Carly paled, when Shadow stepped forward. "I lost my boot, remember," he growled. "We talked about this. You saw my boot."

Carly crab walked to the detectives and looked up. "I think I'd like to go to jail now," she told them.

They stared at her for a minute stunned, then doubled over laughing. "Best job ever," one of them sputtered. "We got permanently assigned to this area," the other laughed. "Once we get her booked, we're free all week, we can't wait to see who gets a girl next, and what trouble she's in. Put us on speed dial," one said.

Then they picked up Carly and walked her to the police car. In minutes, they were gone.

"Fucking detectives," Steele said. "I'm hungry, let's go eat. Navaho you cooking," he asked.

"Yep, I'm cooking," Navaho agreed.

Then Carly was forgotten as they all turned and strode back to the clubhouse for breakfast.

Chapter Fifty
Trike

Trike sat beside his girl and watched as she ate a huge breakfast of bacon and eggs. Navaho had outdone himself and put on a huge spread for everyone. The tension was gone, and all the brothers were relaxing and laughing. It had been a long time coming.

Doc came over then and handed Misty a couple pills. "You've eaten well, but we need to get medicine into you," he said. Trike knew they were pain pills, and antibiotics. He watched as his girl grabbed her juice and dutifully swallowed them.

When she was done with her breakfast, she kissed his cheek, and moved away to sit with Ali and Cassie. When those two got together, mischief soon followed, so Trike was a bit apprehensive about Misty joining them.

He turned to Dragon, when the brother sat down beside him, and clapped him on the back.

"They're fine," he laughed. "No one's after them, and no harm will come to them. It's time all three of them relaxed and had fun," he stated.

"It's the fun, that I'm afraid of," Trike said. "Those three have been through hell, and I'm just worried about what they'll do, now that they know we all have their backs."

Dragon snickered. "Time will tell," he said.

Then they both watched, as the three girls got up, and left the room giggling. Fifteen minutes later they were back, and Ali was carrying a large box. They stood at the bar, and the brothers laughed, as Cassie whistled to get everyone's attention. The room was packed as most of the brothers had been present to witness the punishments.

"Doc," Misty yelled across the room. "Can you come up here for a minute?" Doc looked completely embarrassed as he stood and crossed the room. Ali took over then.

"We wanted to let you know how important you are to us all," she said. "You've dropped everything to help each of us when we needed medical attention. We won't forget your kind words, and the careful way you handled us girls. We love you Doc," she stated. Then each of the girls hugged him and kissed his cheek.

"We talked to Preacher," Cassie said. "We know you don't ride, and we know you have a life outside of the club, but we wanted to do something special for you." Then she moved to the box and opened it up. Misty moved forward next.

"We want to present you with a cut, that declares you an honorary member of The Stone Knight's. You're part of this family, and we want you to know it," she said.

Ali brought the new cut out of the box and helped Doc slip it on. As soon as it was, the entire room erupted into cheers. Doc looked at the bikers with tears in his eyes. He then looked down at the name Doc, that someone had sewn in place.

"Thank you," he said as he fought to regain his composure. "I've never belonged to anything before. It's an honour to be a part of this club, no matter what respect it's in. I promise to wear this cut with pride, and I will treasure it for the rest of my life."

Then all three girls rushed him at once and engulfed Doc in a hug. The man looked as if they had just handed him the world.

"Did you know about this," Trike asked Steele, as he sat down beside them.

"Nope," Steele answered. "It looks like the girls are taking over," he smirked.

"Can't say that isn't a good thing though," Dragon said. "I've never seen that old man happier."

Then Trike outright laughed, as the three girls hurried over to them, and dropped down in each of their laps. All three brothers immediately pulled each girl closer.

"Did we do good," Misty asked him.

"Yeah pretty girl," Trike told her. "You three did real good." Then all three brothers kissed their girls, and the rest of the room erupted into cheers again.

Chapter Fifty One
Misty

Misty was walking beside Brody, and she had no idea where they were headed. He said it was a surprise. She had asked why he didn't blindfold her, but he only got mad, and growled that he would never put her in darkness again. After loosing her sight, and then being trapped in the blackness of the mine, she couldn't agree more.

They headed down the back of the compound, towards the lake. When they got close, Misty stopped and stared in awe. The lake was beautiful, and woods surrounded it, but what had her stopped her, were the three cabins. They sat on the side of the lake, and they were far enough apart, that they were completely private.

Brody grabbed her hand, and she laughed, as he pulled her along behind him. He walked slowly, knowing her leg was bad, then finally turned and scooped her up. They passed the first cabin, and it surprised her to see Ali and Dragon standing on the porch. Ali was jumping up and down on the porch and waving. Misty giggled and waved back.

The next cabin they passed, had Cassie and Steele standing on the porch. Cassie was waving like a madwoman until Steele grabbed her and kissed her. Misty and Brody laughed as Cassie forgot all about them. When they reached the last cabin, Brody stopped and put her down.

"I wish I had my camera," she told him. "This is so pretty," she stated. "Who lives here," she asked in confusion.

Brody smiled down at her. "We do pretty girl," he told her. Then he got down on one knee and looked up at her.

"The first time I saw you, at the lake the night, I fell in love with you. You couldn't see me, and you were scared, but you followed me to my bike and climbed on. You fill my life with meaning, and you make me happier than I've ever been. Will you marry me pretty girl," he asked.

"Yes," she cried, as she threw herself into his arms. "Oh my god, yes."

Then she turned, as clapping, whistling and hollering came from behind them. Standing there were, Ali and Dragon, Cassie and Steele, and her brother. She smiled at them as tears rolled down her face. Then she laughed as Noah picked her up and spun her around.

"I'm happy for you monkey," he said. Then he put her down as the girls rushed her. When she turned to Brody, it was to see him surrounded by the men, and getting half hugs. The girls giggled and hugged her, then turned and ran at Brody. He laughed as they tackled him to the ground.

"Hey," both Steele and Dragon yelled. Then they turned as one, and sandwiched her between them.

"Get away from her fuckers," Brody yelled, as he pushed up off the ground and headed for them.

"Paybacks a bitch," they both said, as they laughed at him, when he punched them in the shoulder.

Once they were all gone, Brody picked her up again, and carried her inside the cabin. When he set her down, she could look around. The cabin was decorated in lots of blues, with yellow accents, and she fell in love with it.

"This is our home," she asked in amazement.

"Yeah pretty girl," Brody told her. "You can change anything you want, I wasn't sure what you liked," he said.

"It's perfect," she told him. "I won't change a thing," she said, as she continued to look around.

"Want to see the bedroom," he asked, as he winked at her.

"I'd love to see the bedroom," she told him shyly. Then she laughed as he grabbed her hand and hauled her down the hall.

She ended up seeing the bedroom, and a lot more, and she loved every minute. They stayed in the cabin all night and didn't come out until the next afternoon.

Chapter Fifty Two
Misty

Misty could only watch Trike as she laid on the bed. He undressed slowly, and she smiled at how handsome he was. When he lifted his head to look at her, it surprised her to see he still had his boxers on.

"You forgot something," she pointed out helpfully. Then she giggled when he smirked at her.

"I need to get you caught up pretty girl," he told her. She watched in anticipation as he prowled towards her. He helped her remove the sling first. "You can do without this for a little while," he said, as he winked at her. "You still have a bad arm and you were shot a little while ago, so no acrobatics for you. Tonight we go slow and easy. Next week we can bring in the sex swing and set it up."

She stared at him in shock, not sure how to take what he said. He looked so serious. Suddenly, he threw his head back and laughed. She blinked as she looked up at him.

"I'm fucking kidding," he told her. She relaxed and leaned forward to smack him on the shoulder.

"You're unbelievable," she giggled.

"Fine," he sighed. "We'll build up to that."

She tilted her head to the side and tried to picture it.

"Jesus," Trike said. "You're fucking thinking about it."

The next thing she knew, she was up, and her shirt and long skirt were gone. He slowly took off her underwear, then he stared at her.

"Your fucking beautiful," he told her as he laid her back down in the middle of the bed. She watched as he removed the boxers and joined her. Then the warmth of his body covered hers.

They took more time learning each other's bodies. Every kiss and every touch was done slowly and with care. They worshipped each other, and she loved it. When he finally entered her for the first time, he stopped and looked down at her.

"I never dreamed I'd have a girl as special as you," he told her. "I've watched Dragon and Steele fall in love, and I've envied their relationships. Now I know what they have because I have it with you. I love you pretty girl, and I promise to be yours forever. I'll love you, I'll keep you safe, and I'll give you everything I can. I love you Misty."

She smiled up at him as tears streamed down her face. "When my parents died, I thought I'd never feel love again. I had my brother, and I do love him, but he had his own life. When I met you it was like everything clicked. You gave me the love I was missing from the moment you met me. With you by my side, I feel like I can do anything. I love you Brody," she told him.

They spent the rest of the night making love, and she loved every minute. It was a long time before they fell asleep, and they both did it with smiles on their faces.

It had only seemed like only a few minutes when she felt Brody shaking her gently and calling her name.

"What time is it," she questioned him sleepily.

"It's just before six," he told her. She glared at him, then pulled the sheets over her head. He laughed at her and pulled them back down.

"Come on sleepy head," he said. Then he lifted her out from the under the sheets and helped her get on some sweats. She was surprised to see he was already dressed.

"Why are we up so early," she asked him curiously.

"You'll see," was all he would say. He was practically bouncing on his feet as he led her out the sliding doors and onto the back deck.

She stopped cold when she saw her tripod and camera set up on the deck, facing the sun that had just started rising over the lake. She starting crying as she tried to take it all in.

"Stop crying silly girl, you're gonna miss it all," he said, as he wiped at her tears with the corner of his shirt.

"I love you so much," she said as she hurried to the camera.

"I love you too," Brody answered, as he parked it in a deck chair. He spent the next hour watching her take pictures, and she finally felt like she had everything she could ever want.

Chapter Fifty Three
Trike

Three days later, Trike was in heaven. Things with Misty were amazing. She was getting more confidence; she was laughing and smiling all the time, and she was never far from him or her brother. Trike loved how close they were and figured the two years apart had made them even closer. Noah was just as protective of her as he was, Misty just shook her head and humoured them. Trike had a feeling, that after living with Carly for so long, she loved the attention.

Trike loved waking up with his fiancé in his arms. He now understood why Steele and Dragon were so possessive. If anybody even looked at his girl too long, he turned into a monster.

Misty had also began to take pictures again, and it thrilled Trike. In the three days since she had moved in, the brothers had helped him build a shed, that she could use as a darkroom. She told Trike what chemicals and equipment she needed, and him and Cassie went out to get it. Trike bought the basics, then Cassie bought a years supply. She planned on giving it to Misty as a wedding gift.

Trike had told Misty that in a weeks time, he was marrying her. He got the same justice of the peace that had married Ali and Dragon, and they were planning to tie the knot beside the cabin. He told her that it would be small, and intimate, and that it would be casual. Trike wanted to wear jeans and his cut, but he didn't care what she wore. She easily agreed with that. Misty said that without her parents; she didn't need a big production. He didn't like that answer, so he would make sure it was special for her.

He had also helped Noah clean out the locker, over the last couple days. Everything that was Carly's was bagged up and carted to the dump. Noah left most of his stuff there, seeing as his room in the clubhouse was small. Trike gathered the last of Misty's stuff and stored it in the cabin.

Then Noah surprised him, by giving him their mothers wedding rings. Apparently, after the accident, Noah had taken them and put them away. Misty had no idea he even had them. Trike was thankful and made sure Noah knew it. Apparently, Noah was keeping his dad's rings for when he got married. Trike hoped he didn't have to wait too long. The man deserved to be happy too. He just hoped Carly hadn't messed him up too much.

Trike was happy too, to see Noah had made a good friend. He and Shadow had become close, and the men were found together often. With them both having a military background, the friendship wasn't a surprise. Trike knew both brothers would be huge assets to the club.

Doc had also become the surrogate father of all the girls. Ali's father had died, Misty's father had died, and Cassie wanted nothing to do with hers. Doc seemed to be thriving since he joined the club, and Trike was happy for the old man.

The detectives had stopped by, and announced that Carly was sentenced to life in prison, with no chance of parole. The prison doctors had looked at her eyes, and they figured it would take months to heal. It would make her first few months in prison extremely difficult, and the club couldn't be happier.

To celebrate, the club had a huge barbecue and fire tonight, and Trike couldn't wait. He planned to give Misty her mom's engagement ring, as he didn't have one when he proposed. Things were going good, but he couldn't wait until the wedding was over, then Misty would be his in every way possible.

Chapter Fifty Four
Misty

Misty was bouncing on her feet, as she stood in the shop, staring in the mirror. She had found the perfect dress. Brody wanted the wedding to be casual. He wanted to wear his jeans, boots and cut. Misty didn't mind at all, she figured it would be more fun that way.

They planned to have the ceremony beside the cabins, down at the lake. They wanted to do it in the early evening, just as the sun was going down, and then have a big fire to celebrate. Misty was thrilled with that, she wasn't one who liked a lot of attention, so Trike had considered that.

The bikers were attending, along with Mario, and it surprised her to find out the two detectives would be there too. They were coming around increasingly and had helped the club out frequently.

"That dress looks fantastic on you," Cassie told her. "You have to let me buy it for you," she squealed.

Misty smiled at her new friend, then turned to Ali. "What do you think," she asked her.

"I think Trike's gonna haul you off as soon as the ceremonies over," she giggled. Both Misty and Cassie laughed with her, knowing that was most likely what would happen.

The dress was white, but was more in the style of a sundress, then a wedding dress. It had spaghetti straps and a tight-fitting bodice, then it fell to her knees.

"This is definitely the dress," she told the girls. "I love it."

"Then go get changed, and we'll get it," Cassie declared.

Two stores later, and the girls found their bridesmaid dresses. They were sundresses as well, but were in a pretty blue flowery pattern. They looked perfect on the girls.

Misty had asked them to stand up with her, the night Trike proposed, and they had both said yes. Brody had asked Dragon and Steele to stand up with him, so it was working out unbelievably well.

The girls made their purchases and hurried back to the compound. The barbecue would start soon, and they didn't want to be late. The barbecue was a combination engagement party and bachelor party. They stored their dresses at Cassie's and walked back across the grass.

When the men saw the girls, they each broke away to greet them. Misty laughed as Brody picked her up and spun her around. Then he kissed her senseless before placing her back on her feet.

"Did you girls find some dresses," he asked.

"We did," Misty replied, and would have said more, but Preacher interrupted.

"Now the girls are fucking here, we can start," he teased. "Misty, Trike, come up here a second would you." They both made their way over to him. "Congratulations you two, I wish you the best." Then Trike thanked him and turned back to her.

"I didn't have a ring for you when I proposed, so I think we need to fix that," he said. Then he took her hand and slipped a ring on her finger.

She looked down and gasped as she saw her mothers ring sitting on her finger. She had forgotten all about it. Tears pooled in her eyes and dropped down her cheeks.

"How," she whispered.

"I had help," he told her, as he pointed out Noah. Her brother smiled at her and winked. She crossed over to him and jumped into his arms.

"Thank you," she said happily.

"You're welcome," he said as he kissed her head. "Love you monkey."

"Love you too," she said, then she ran back over to Brody and flung herself at him. He laughed as he caught her and pulled her close.

The rest of the night went off without a hitch. The group drank and laughed and enjoyed themselves. Preacher even surprised Shadow by patching him in.

Apparently, you were supposed to wait a year before becoming a fully patched member, but Shadow had proven himself, so the club cut the prospects time in half. Shadow looked like they had handed him the holy grail as he put on his new cut, to a loud round of applause.

Preacher also presented Noah with a prospect cut, and told him that if all went well, he would also be patched in within the next six months. With everything that had happened with the other prospects, the club knew to grab the good ones when they saw them.

The night had been perfect, but Misty couldn't wait for her wedding in the next couple days.

Chapter Fifty Five
Trike

Two days later, it was almost time for Misty to walk down the isle. The brothers had built a beautiful arch out of wood, and they had decorated it in vines and tiny lights. They placed it right beside the lake, and with the sun setting, it was stunning. They had also hung paper lanterns in the trees. Trike hope Misty liked it as he wanted it to be special for her.

Trike stood in front of the arch, with Steele and Dragon. They all wore jeans, a black t-shirt and their cuts. All the brothers in the club were present, along with Mario and his right-hand man Trent, and the two detectives Tripp Jamison and Darren Macks. It had been kind of funny to learn their names after calling them the detectives for so long.

The detectives actually turned out to be good guys. They had helped them out and even covered up for them. When the club had taken out Keith, the detectives turned a blind eye, and they completely ignored the foot comment from Carly. Trike wouldn't actually call them crooked, but it was nice to have a couple friends on the force.

Navaho started the wedding march song, and it softly sounded, from the speakers the brother had placed among the trees. Trike craned his neck, trying to see down the isle. The girls had gotten ready in Cassie's cabin, as it was closest. He heard a door shut, and then he saw his girl.

She appeared at the beginning of the isle, on her brothers arm. Noah looked proud, as he walked towards them with his new prospect cut on, and his sister at his side. He was glad Noah made home in time to be here although he was sure Doc would have taken his place if he wasn't.

His eyes were drawn to his bride though. She looked amazing in her pretty white dress. Unfortunately, she still had her sling on, and she still limped from the gunshot wound, but Trike didn't care. The dress had tiny spaghetti straps, a fitted top, and a flowing skirt.

Her hair had been curled, and they had pinned the sides up, so it was out of her face, the rest fell softly down her back. She had tiny white sandals on her feet.

For her something blue, Trike knew she had a blue garter on under her dress, Dragon had happily spilled the beans on that one. For her something borrowed, she wore a pair of Cassie's diamond earrings. And, for something new, Trike had given her a necklace that had an affinity charm dangling from it.

When she finally reached Trike, Noah kissed her cheek, and shook his hand. Then he laughed and stepped back, as Trike grabbed his bride to be, hauled her against his chest, and kissed her. Hoots and laughter followed, until the minister tapped him on the should, and told him he was supposed to wait until the end. He ignored him, and turned to the front, tucking Misty into his side, so the ceremony could start.

The wedding went quickly, but Trike would remember every second, for the rest of his life. Misty had cried, when Trike had produced her mothers wedding ring, and it had taken a minute to calm her. Then the ceremony was over, and once again Trike got to kiss her, but this time it was as his wife.

The bikers had laughed again, when Trike picked her up, and carried her to their cabin. He kept her there for two hours before they returned to the party. Trike blamed it all on the dress, but honestly he just loved his wife, and wanted to show her how happy he was.

The party went until early the next morning, but Trike only lasted about four hours, until he was dragging her off again. And that time, they didn't return.

Epilogue

The end of the wedding had been pandemonium. Preacher had gotten a phone call telling him his baby sister had been kidnapped. Nobody told Trike until the next day, wanting him to enjoy his wedding night. The club was getting ready for a war, as it was The Outlaws, that had taken her. They were the same club that had kidnapped Dragon's woman, Ali. Shadow had taken it upon himself, to ride in and free her, and Trike wished the brother luck. If anyone could do it, it would be him.

Trike had been grateful that the brothers had kept him out of it. His night with Misty had been perfect. They drank champagne; they made love, and they laughed. Misty even got out pictures of her family and shared things about her childhood with him.

Then she had cried when he pulled out the cut he had made for her. She had thrown herself at him when she saw her new club name was Monkey. Trike had explained that since he called her by so many endearments that he asked Noah if he could use his. Noah had agreed, honoured that his nickname would become official.

They talked about children and discovered that they both wanted three. Now that Misty could see, she wanted to get started right away, and Trike didn't have a problem with that. He told her that they could always add on to the cabin if they needed it, the more the merrier.

When Misty said she may already be pregnant, because the meds she was taking might have made her pills ineffective, Trike went a little crazy. He snatched up her champagne and poured it down the drain, then ran for the car keys. She caught him before he reached the door, explaining that a pregnancy test could wait until tomorrow. Trike pouted, but carried her back to bed. Two weeks later, Misty took the test, and it was positive!

The club was growing, babies were coming, and tension was mounting. It looked like Mario had found a woman, and it was hilarious to watch his mood swings, and craziness. Tripp, one of the detectives, was involved with someone, and of course she came with a crazy step brother. Then Shadow had gone after Preachers sister, and was due back soon, with gun toting bikers on his tail.

Things with the club would never be boring, but then again life never was. You take the good with the bad and push through it, and if that doesn't work, there's always pink bedding to lift the mood.

About the Author

MEGAN FALL is a mother of three who helps her husband run his construction business. She has been writing all her life, but with a push from her daughter, started publishing. It's the best thing she ever did. When she's not writing, you can find her at the beach. She loves searching for rocks, sea glass, driftwood and fossils. She believes in ghosts, collects ridiculous amounts of plants, and rides on the back of her hubby's motorcycle.

MEGAN FALL

Look for these books coming soon!

STONE KNIGHTS MC SERIES
Finding Ali
Saving Cassie
Loving Misty
Rescuing Tiffany
Guarding Alexandria
Protecting Fable
Surviving November
Sheltering Macy
Defending Zoe

DEVILS SOLDIERS MC SERIES
Resisting Diesel
Surviving Hawk

THE ENFORCER SERIES
The Enforcer
The Enforcers Revenge

Rescuing Tiffany
Stone Knight's Book 4

Chapter One
Shadow

The wedding had been beautiful. No matter what the brothers said, to rile Trike up, the smile never left his face. He was an extremely happy biker. And, Misty had been a stunning bride. Her white sundress had fit her perfectly, and she wore the prettiest blush all night, as the brothers teased her.

Shadow was happy for the couple. Misty had been through hell. Her brothers girlfriend had tried to kill her, on two separate occasions. The first, was when Misty was still blind, and the girlfriend moved the furniture, so the poor girl fell into a glass coffee table. And the second time, was when she shot her and blew up a mine, trapping her inside.

Both times Trike had saved her, and now that the threat was eliminated, they could enjoy their time together. Shadow was glad Misty joined the club, because with her came her brother, Noah. Noah had quickly become the brother he was closest to. Both had served in the military, and both were around the same age. Of all the brothers here, he trusted Noah the most.

The last year had been hard on him. He had joined the navy fresh out of high school, and he had loved it. He trained hard and quickly passed the Navy Seal requirements. From there, they had drafted him into a secret branch of the seals. He was known as a Shadow Warrior, and his team could slip in and out of places, undetected.

After five years of that, he was done. He loved his job, and he loved his seal brothers, but the time had come to move on. He knew it was only a matter of time before he was killed in the line of duty. Unfortunately, he had watched many seals die over the years, and he didn't plan to be one of them.

So, for the last year, he had packed a bag, hopped on his Harley, and ridden all over the country. He loved the freedom of the open road, and he loved having no one to answer to even more. But after a while, he decided it was time to find somewhere new to belong. He missed his seal brothers, and he missed the family type relationship they provided.

Three months later, he stopped at a bar, and met Preacher. The man was a bit older than him, but they got along like long lost best friends. Shadow was amazed by the instant friendship that started that day. When he found out Preacher was the president of The Stone Knight's MC, he decided to check it out.

That evening, he became a prospect, and found himself engulfed in a new family. Six months later, he was a fully patched in member. Apparently, most prospects were patched in after a year, but Shadow had proven himself. Plus, with his military background, the brothers decided to cut the probation period in half. And Shadow couldn't be happier.

The wedding was long over now, and there were only about half the brothers wandering around, when Preacher's cell rang. The brothers all stopped talking, to glance his way.

"Preacher," the president growled into the phone. "I'm at a wedding, what the hell do you want?" Then there was silence as the man waited for whoever was on the other end to speak again.

"What," Preacher suddenly bellowed, as he threw his bottle as hard as he could, against the gravel surrounding the fire pit. Then there were rapid fire questions as the brothers looked on in concern.

How long, which direction, and how many men, were growled from Preacher. Then he turned off his phone and roared up at the sky. The brothers stared at Preacher in shock. The man was always calm and controlled, so this meant something was seriously wrong.

"My baby sisters been kidnapped," he finally shared. "I'm leaving in the next fifteen minutes, to rip out the throats of everyone that took her. Anybody that wants can go with me, if they can keep up," he sneered, as he turned and headed for the clubhouse.

The brothers looked at each other in shock, then tore off after their president. Shadow had no idea, that his next decision, was going to completely change his life.